DREAM WALKING
IN MY STRIPEY
WORLD

To Anne
I hope you feel better soon,
and I hope you enjoy my book.
Love Yvone xxx

D1336163

Pavon James

ISBN: 978-1-910205-62-4

Printed and Published by:
For the Right Reasons,
60 Grant St Inverness IV3 8BS
fortherightreasons@rocketmail.com

Reviews

"This book took me back to my favourite childhood book (Enid Blyton's "The Far Away Tree") This book was escapism with a very well written message through it."

R. Hansen

"A great read and insight from a child's perspective of a harrowing family life, that's unfortunately more common in this present day, written with coping mechanisms for the children that were excellent."

F. Mackenzie

"An excellent read that has been brilliantly written from a young person's perspective offering inspiration, motivation and hope in every page."

S. Dyer

CONTENTS

Preface

Five years ago I went home from work at the end of a shift, very frustrated, having worked with another of the numerous families that I've worked with over the years who were living with domestic abuse and too afraid to speak out. As a result of their fear of disclosing, I was unable to do anything to help them. I sat that evening questioning whether or not I was in the right job. I found myself starting to write and that writing became the book you hold in your hand today. A large part of my frustration was seeing the impact the abuse had on children. Whilst many parents believed that they were hiding the abuse and violence from them, because they were not in the same room when it happened, they were unaware of the trauma caused whilst their children saw and heard much more than they realised.

I decided that if children were going to be have to live in those conditions and I was unable to help them anymore, then I could offer them some coping mechanisms through this book. The book is written through the eyes of an eleven-year-old girl and takes the main character and her younger brother to a fantasy world (the World Of Light) where they are taught these coping mechanisms, which they can put into practice in real life. In fact, these coping mechanisms can be used for anybody going through any difficult situation.

This book is aimed at children over the age of eleven years old, however the older generation will also appreciate this book, which deals with a difficult subject in a light manner, with the use of humour.

Acknowledgements

I wish to thank everyone for all their amazing support and help in the creation of this book. Special acknowledgements are on page 227 for some of the people who truly inspired supported and encouraged me through the creation of this book.

Dedication

This book is dedicated to Jimmy and Eileen for helping me be the person I am today. Thank you both for showing me the right path in life, for without your acceptance, support, guidance, love and care I would not be who I am today. I love you both.

To Jonathan for giving me the opportunity to be a Mum to an amazing son, who has never failed to inspire me or bring me smiles in each day. I am so proud of you. I love you more than life itself.

To my amazing husband, Paul, for not only being my soulmate and twin flame but for loving me the way you do. You are my inspiration and tower of strength every day. Thank you for believing me in and in this book, you are my rock. I love you.

To all the animals that I have been so blessed to share my life with. You are the place I find solace and tranquillity. Thank you for your unconditional love. I love you all.

To all the beautiful children who are growing up in abusive situations today. This book is for you. Be proud of who you are and know that you are stronger than you think.

Prologue

Dawn heard the screaming and shouting again. She saw her Dad take a second can of beer from the fridge and knew it was going to be another one of those nights. It happened most nights but it was always worse the nights that he drank beer. She knew that her Mum knew too, because she wouldn't sit down the nights he'd have beer. She would run after him constantly asking him if he wanted his slippers or if he wanted dinner or the TV switched on. She always tried to please him.

CHAPTER ONE

You'd think she would have realised by now that she'll never please him no matter what she does. For crying out loud, I'm 11 years old and *I* can work that much out! I've been able to see it for years so why can't she see it? I don't know why she won't just pack our things and let us run away from him. I've asked her to do that so many times but all she ever says is there's no point because he would find us. I don't believe her. I think if we ran away far enough he would never find us and we would all be safe forever.

I'd found my safe place for now. I didn't have enough time to run and hide in my bedroom so I squeezed into the tiny space behind the couch. When Dad's been drinking he forgets where I hide. I keep telling Mum to find a safe place, just as she constantly reminds us to do, but she just tells me she's okay. She must think I'm stupid because I know she's not okay. I know she's terrified but she'll never admit that. It's always, "Dawn its fine, your Dad doesn't mean to hurt me," or "Dawn, your Dad just needs help" and the best one is, "Dawn, your Dad loves me."

Love! Well, if that's what love feels like I never want anybody to love me in my whole life – not ever.

1

He may put his arms around her and cuddle her sometimes but that doesn't mean he loves her, because five minutes later he'll be throwing something at her, punching and kicking her. I can't bear it. I hate knowing he's hurting her, that's why I hide. But I can still hear it, I hear him using the ugliest words and I hear the slaps and punches while he tells Mum how useless she is and how it's her own fault.

Mum screams and cries how sorry she is and she always promises to try harder for him, but I don't know why. When she looks in the mirror the next day and sees her face is all bruised and cut she cries. She doesn't know I hear or see her, but I do. So how can she tell me she loves him? I don't understand adults! She tells me when I grow up one day I'll be away from it all and I'll understand that it's not as easy as just walking away. She's right, I don't understand. Why Mum? Why wait all those years of crying and being hurt, why can't we run away from him now? I've thought about running away on my own but I'm too scared Dad will kill her and I need to be there to protect her and cuddle her to tell her it will all be okay.

Just as I'd expected, I heard the screams starting again and I knew that he was pulling her hair and dragging her across the room. I got to know what each different scream meant and I knew that one. Next he'd throw her on the couch and the punching would start. I tried not to breathe too noisily and I stayed so still, as if I was playing musical statues. I couldn't risk Dad knowing I was there.

He never really hits me, not much, sometimes he'd slap me but that was it. It wasn't like the slaps Mum got, but I was still scared. If he knew I was there Mum would get it worse. I did get caught once and got told to get to my room. I heard him screaming at Mum that she was a useless mother "What kind of mother lets their child see her in that state?" he'd scream at her. After the punching and screaming stopped Dad would often sit and drink more beer. He didn't just hit her when he was drinking, but it was always worse when he had been.

Sometimes he'd tell me the next day how much he loved me, and that I was his little princess, sometimes he'd come into my room late at night to tell me and he would be stinking of drink. I hated it when he was like that because I knew the screaming and shouting could start again anytime. He'd tell me my Mum needs to learn how to be a wife. Sometimes he'd drag her upstairs to their bedroom and I'd really hear her screaming. I hated my Dad for hurting her. I hated what he did and I hated him being in our house. Sometimes I'd feel guilty thinking that way, because he'd be really nice to me and take me to the park and buy me sweets and I'd wonder if Mum really *was* a bad wife and that's maybe just what happened if you weren't a good wife. I just knew I didn't like hearing it or seeing her so messed up on her face. He never used to leave bruises on her face, it was always somewhere she could hide them, but recently he's just hit her anywhere. It's like he doesn't care.

The punching eventually stopped and I heard Mum sobbing on the couch and Dad going to the fridge for more beer, so I waited until the beer made him fall asleep and I could hear him snoring and I crept upstairs to my bedroom.

My bedroom was my safe place. Mum had always told us to make sure that we had somewhere safe we could go when Dad went off on one. We used to be able to run to our neighbour's house as the lady there was my Mums friend. But Dad said that Mum's friend was a bad influence on all of us and he didn't like us going to her house. Eventually Dad fell out with all our neighbours and nobody will speak to us now. We had nobody that we could run to, or talk to, so Danny and I used our bedrooms as our safe place. Sometimes if I was too slow in getting to the stairs to get up to my room I'd hide behind the couch. Dad has never caught me there so it was a safe place for me, but the safest place to be was always in my bedroom. Dad rarely ever came up to our rooms when he was having a go at Mum. If I did hear him come upstairs I would hide in my bedroom cupboard, behind my clothes, but most of the time when he did come up he'd go into his bedroom and I'd not see him.

When I got to my bedroom, I went straight to the vent. The vent is a big square hole in the wall where the heating comes out and it has a kind of grill over the front of it, but I can see through the vent to my little brother's bedroom. Danny's only eight years old and he's always terrified when Dad goes off on one. As soon as Dad comes home Danny runs to his bedroom and just stays there, and if I make it to my bedroom before Dad kicks off I speak to Danny through the vent to try and stop him feeling so scared. He'll rarely come into my room because Dad tells him to act like a man and not be frightened as he is only teaching Mum how to be a good wife. Danny was too scared for me to go through to his room in case Dad thought he wasn't being a man. We called the vent "Amitola" because that's where we always wished dreams could come true - to escape from the shouting and fighting. Amitola means rainbow and I named it this after speaking to Danny one day through the vent when he was sad and I sang to him to cheer him up. The only words of the song I could remember were "somewhere over the rainbow skies are blue and dreams can come true." When I sang it to him it made him smile and we had called it the Amitola ever since. I was glad I listened to the teacher when she taught us about the Native Americans or I'd never have known that word existed, which also meant we could use it without Mum or Dad knowing what we were talking about.

I tapped the Amitola three times. Three taps is the code that I'm in my bedroom on my own and want to speak to him. Two taps would have told him that I'd made it back to my own room and I was okay – I usually use that one when I've been hiding in my safe place so Danny knows I've made it to my room safely. One tap means Mum or Dad is in my room or near one of our rooms.

After I tapped, Danny came to the Amitola. His face was red and soaking wet with tears, like it usually is after the fighting starts.

"Are you okay, Danny?" I asked.

"I just wish they'd stop, I'm so scared," he replied in the sad way he always did. I knew he felt scared and I did too, but I couldn't let Danny see that. I had to be strong for him. I persuaded him to go to his bed and that it would be okay in the morning.

I closed the vent and stood looking out of my bedroom window. I could see the kids in the street playing and laughing. They looked happy and seemed to be having so much fun. I wouldn't dream of playing outside, not that I'd ever be allowed and if I did ever go out and Dad caught me, well it just wouldn't be worth it.

I could still hear the fighting downstairs and felt myself getting more upset as I heard it at the same time I heard the giggling of normal kids playing outside. I could feel the anger building inside of me. "It's so unfair" I complained to myself as the tears rolled down my cheeks. I threw my clothes off and got into bed. I couldn't watch them play any longer. Why, oh why, oh why? What did I ever do so wrong? I could still hear them playing outside so I got up and closed my curtains, refusing to look. I'd seen and heard enough to know they were having fun and I'd never be part of it. I threw myself into my bed, feeling sorry for myself. It wasn't often that I felt sorry for myself, but tonight I did.

I lay in bed and tried to fall asleep so I could forget about them, but it didn't work and no matter how hard I tried not to hear them it was all I could hear. With each minute that passed I felt myself getting more upset until eventually I put my fingers in my ears to block out the noise of them playing. All of a sudden a bright white light, the brightest light I'd ever seen, appeared from nowhere. I pulled the covers up to the top of my nose as I heard a voice "Do not be afraid Dawn, I am here to help you."

What was that light? Who was that speaking and what did they want? I rubbed my eyes, opening them wide again, but the bright light was still there. I nipped my arm to see if I was properly awake. Ouch! Yip, I was definitely awake and the bright light was still there.

I squeaked, "Who's there?"

Suddenly the bright light became millions of different coloured stars. There were reds, oranges, blues, greens and other bright colours. All of these stars fell in front of me and from the middle of them emerged the most beautiful array of colours in the shape of a butterfly. It was the most beautiful thing I'd ever seen and for some reason I didn't feel scared anymore. Instead I felt calm and somehow safe. I didn't know what this was or what it wanted but I wasn't afraid. I felt like I ought to be, but I just wasn't. The butterfly had huge wings and it wasn't a normal sized butterfly, it was more like the size of a bird yet I still wasn't scared. I just lay there mesmerised by the beautiful colours and peaceful feeling it brought with it. Each wing was a beautiful purple and pink swirling around each other and in between the wings looked like a tiny person – like a girl with blonde hair which was nearly as long as she was, wearing a lilac t-shirt, a little pink tutu skirt and black and white spotted tights with no shoes on. As I was trying to absorb what I was seeing I heard a voice that sounded like an angel "My name is Mirabriel." I'd never seen or heard an angel before, but that's what I imagined one would sound like. Her voice was calming. "Do not be afraid, I am here to help you and Danny."

I lay very still until I managed to ask, "How do you know my name? Who are you? Why are you here?" My mind was racing with different thoughts. But with all of these thoughts I never once thought she was going to hurt me or was here to harm me. I can't explain why but I just knew there was nothing to be frightened of.

"So many questions to answer, my precious child!" Mirabriel said, with love and care in her voice. "For now, all you need to know is that I am your protector and I am going to be around you to help you feel safe. When you feel sad, know that I am here. You won't always be able to see me, but I'll be here. In time I will tell you how you can ask to see me when you need to but for now just know that I am here for you."

There was so much to take in. I knew I was awake but I nipped my leg again to make sure. Ouch! There was no doubt, I was definitely awake. But what is a protector? Why would anybody want to make *me* feel safe? How did she know my name? Did that mean that I did something to make her appear? There were so many thoughts in my head. I was about to ask her when she said, "Precious child, sometimes you think too much. I promise you that you will understand much more as time goes on and as you get to know me."

Without meaning to I yelped out loud, "Wow! You heard my thoughts?" and Mirabriel let out the funniest giggle and told me that she had to go.

"Please stay," I begged her even though I was still trying to work out why I felt so safe around this very strange yet beautiful......butterfly? But butterflies don't speak. Thing?......Woman? Was she a woman? What was it?

"I am a Frangel" she replied "I have the energy of a Fairy and an Angel mixed together" she continued "I am your guardian Frangel and I am here to protect you, guide you and make sure no harm comes to you. You have nothing to be afraid of, I will cause you no harm. Nobody else can see me, unless you want them to see me - I am your very own invisible friend. Please get some sleep dear child and we will talk more tomorrow."

Fairy? Angel? Frangel? What on earth was going on? Everyone says fairies and angels don't exist. I was so confused but I knew I loved her being here. I didn't want her to leave, I wanted to sit in that peaceful feeling forever. I'd never felt quite so unafraid of anything in my life – I wasn't even afraid of Mum or Dad whilst Mirabriel was there. In fact, I even forgot that they were fighting downstairs.

All of a sudden the light that Mirabriel was surrounded by turned from white to gold. She was so beautiful. She reminded me of a rag doll that I had when I was younger, without the wings. Her outfit matched her skin perfectly and she had the brightest green eyes - so kind and gentle looking. Her wings were more beautiful than I could describe. If I hadn't seen her in the middle of the wings, I'd have said she was the most beautiful butterfly I'd ever seen but she wasn't a butterfly. She was a lady. No wait a minute, she was a fringel......no a fangabel......arrrgghh what was it? A fairyangel?......a fire angel? As the white light changed to gold Mirabriel said, "My dear Dawn, I am a Frangel and I am leaving you now with a sprinkling of rainbow stars to help keep you safe until I return," and with that I found myself in a shower of coloured stars and coloured powder stuff....rainbow stars were everywhere.

Mirabriel became brighter and brighter until all I could see was the same bright light that she had arrived in with lots of coloured stars floating around her. Then the coloured stars joined together and formed an astonishingly beautiful rainbow. It was

9

majestic in every way, made up of every colour I knew a rainbow had – red, yellow, green, blue, indigo, violet and orange. As the rainbow became perfectly formed Mirabriel disappeared. It was as if she had melted into the rainbow and both Mirabriel and the rainbow vanished, leaving my room in darkness again. It was pitch black and I couldn't see anything. I just lay for what seemed like a long time trying to work out what had just happened.

CHAPTER TWO

I must have fallen fast asleep, because when I woke in the morning I jumped up in excitement as I remembered my visitor the night before. I jumped out of bed and went to gather up all the rainbow stars that the Frangel had poured over me, but there weren't any. I pulled my covers back excitedly – nothing. I moved my pillows – nothing. They had to be here somewhere! I moved my sheets – nothing. I looked under my bed – nothing. Just as I was looking under my bed my Mum came into my room.

"What do you think you're doing, Dawn?" she yelled at me. "You're meant to be getting your brother ready for school. He's not even had his breakfast yet and you need to leave in ten minutes." It looked like it was another normal day then, except Mum wasn't usually up at all.

"And tidy up that bedroom before you go," she yelled as she walked away.

I made my bed and felt the tears rolling down my face. I was sad because I'd really believed that at last someone cared enough to come and look after us. She seemed so real. I even remembered hurting my leg when I'd pinched it so I was sure I hadn't been dreaming. I checked my leg and there was a tiny purple mark where I'd nipped it, but I couldn't see any rainbow stars anywhere. I knew she'd poured lots over me – so I guessed it must have been a dream after all. Still, it had been a really good dream to have had. I wiped my tears and told myself to get on with it.

"Come on Danny, we're going to miss the bus," I told him as I grabbed us a banana each for breakfast. On the way to the bus I wanted to find out if Danny had heard anything, without telling him what I'd seen.

"How did you sleep last night?" I asked.

"On my side," was his smart reply.

"Ha-ha, I mean did you wake up through the night at all?"

"No, why?" he asked curiously.

"I was just wondering," I said silently as I tried to work it out in my head.

"Danny, did you see a light in your room last night after we spoke at the Amitola?" I asked without giving anything away.

"No. Why are you asking me all these questions? What did he do last night?" he asked in a worried tone.

"Nothing. I didn't see Dad after I went to bed, I just thought I saw a light on in your room after we spoke. It doesn't matter, I must have imagined it," I reassured him.

"Yeah, you must have," Danny retorted.

As we sat on the bus a piece of scrunched up paper hit Danny on the back of the head. We were used to this type of thing. Just because we didn't have the trendy clothes that the other kids had, they picked on us all the time. They didn't do it in school because Danny and I have a few friends who are really nice to us, and they'd stick up for us, but our friends were never on the bus.

"Oi, pee-pants!" someone shouted from the back of the bus as Danny got hit again.

"Danny don't cry, don't let them win, that's just what they want," I whispered to him as he wiped away the tear that rolled down his cheek.

Danny sat there not saying a word. He was used to being called those kinds of names because he often peed the bed in his sleep. Dad would get so mad when he did it and I once heard Mum telling him it's because Danny was frightened of all the shouting but Dad got mad at Mum when she said it so she never said it again.

It was true though, Danny did smell sometimes but that's because I can't reach the shower to put it on for him. I had tried once and I fell off the stool, smashing my chin off the bath and Mum got mad at me because there was blood everywhere and she was worried about the school finding out about me having to get Danny ready for school, so she told me not to do it again. So Danny had to go to school smelling of pee. It didn't bother me because he's my brother and I love him, even though I do sometimes hate him too but that's only when he annoys me. Like the time he put worms inside my bed and waited to see my reaction, or the time he put farting powder in my juice – though that backfired on him and he was the one who suffered when it took effect! Or when he picks his nose and wipes it on my jumper. Yip, he makes me hate him sometimes but when someone else hurts him or calls him names I don't like it at all.

It was time to get off the bus as we pulled up at the school gates. We both love school, it's our escape from living at home. Peggy and Lola, my two best friends, were waiting at the school gates for me and I ran to meet them with Danny running right behind me. Stu and Fergus were just across the playground and Danny went to join them. School was a fun place for Danny and me, as well as a safe place for us.

Well, *some* days it was fun and we'd both forget what life was really like, but other days it would be really hard because I would want to play with my friends but I'd be scared in case I spoke about what happened at home the night before. That was only when it had been a really bad night though. Mum always told us that if we ever told anybody what went on at home Danny and I would be taken away by social work or the police, so we kept it our secret. Mum and Dad had told us never to trust social work or the police as they were just interfering and wanted to hurt families instead of helping them. They said they would put us with a strange family and Danny and I would never see each other or Mum or Dad again.

I remember the time I went to school with a bruise on my face after I'd been thrown against the living room wall the night before – I had tried to stop Dad hitting Mum, but instead of stopping he just pushed me out of the way and kept hurting her. It was horrible and my face hurt so much that when I went to bed that night Mum told me I couldn't go to school the next day because it was too risky. When I got up in the morning she was still asleep, so I went anyway. The teacher asked me what had happened and I told her that I'd fallen. Later that morning the teacher took me out of class and told me someone wanted to speak to me. I went into a room with two ladies who told me they were from the police and social work and that they wanted to check that I was happy and safe. They told me my teacher was worried about me.

Oh boy, I knew exactly what they wanted. They seemed nice but I wasn't falling for their tricks! I was so glad Mum had warned me. If she hadn't I would probably have talked to them as they did sound as if they cared. I didn't care if they took me away from Dad, but they weren't going to take me away from my Mum. I loved my Mum so much. Who would protect her from him if I wasn't there? No way, I wasn't letting that happen, so I told the ladies that I was safe and when they asked what happened to my face I told them that I'd fallen. I was worried the entire time that I was talking to them, I was so sure that they must have known that I was lying. They said my teacher was worried about me because I'd had a few bruises recently. I really did want to tell them for them to help me, so they could make Mum safe, but Mum had made it clear what would happen if I did, so I said nothing.

Mum wasn't allowed any friends and she certainly wasn't allowed to let them into our house, but I knew she had one because I'd hear her on the phone to her. One day she caught me listening in and begged me not to tell Dad that she had spoken to her friend. I used to wonder why the phone rang once then stopped before ringing again a few seconds later. But I soon realised that it was a code for Mum to know that it was her friend. It happened once when Dad was there and he dialled a number to find out who had called, he went mad on Mum saying it was a withheld number and she must know who it was. I do remember the day that she was extremely brave and she sneaked a friend into the house before Dad got home. I was lugging in through the gap under the door, her friend was trying to persuade her to leave Dad, saying that she would help her escape, but Mum said Dad always threatened to find her and make sure she never saw Danny and I again, so she wouldn't go. Her friend even told her that Women's Aid could give the three of us somewhere safe to stay where Dad couldn't get to us. I didn't know what Women's Aid was but if they could keep us all safe surely that was the answer. But Mum refused to have any of it. She told her friend that she would wait until Danny and I left home before she left him. That seemed like such a long time for her to suffer. For all of us to suffer.

I didn't plan on telling Mum what had happened at school that day, but when I got home she knew anyway. She had been so angry and she'd kept asking me what I'd told them. She eventually believed me when I told her that I hadn't told them anything, and she'd warned me never to tell anybody about our life at home. She could see how upset I was as I begged her to leave. She told me that she had been given a number for someone who could help us all get out of there. When I asked if she had called she just said that she couldn't. I knew why, but I couldn't tell her that I knew or I'd be in trouble for lugging in.

After school, Danny and I got off the school bus and walked home. We never really talk about what happens at home when we're not there, but as we got closer to the house we both saw Dad's car at the same time and without thinking we slowed our pace down, gasping "Oh no!" at exactly the same time. We knew when Dad was home early it usually meant he'd been drinking and it made it much harder to get out of the way when we went in. It usually meant we'd have to sit and have dinner with Mum and Dad at the same time. Family mealtimes were never pleasant and always full of arguments – usually Dad picking arguments with Mum and Mum trying not to cry or get mad back at him in front of us.

As we got closer to the house Danny broke the silence "Do you think we'll make it upstairs before he starts?" He looked so frightened.

"I don't know Danny, but whatever you do just don't wind him up," I replied.

"But…" Danny started, but I knew what he was going to say.

"I know you don't like seeing him being horrible to Mum but trying to stick up for her only makes him worse," I tried to reason with him. We both knew we'd have to sit at the same table as him for our dinner which always filled us with dread, especially when he'd been drinking.

We went into the house and there was no sign of Dad. Mum was in the kitchen, on her own, cooking dinner.

"Did you have a good day at school?" she asked, which was met with a big smile from both of us. She knew we felt safe at school. "*If* you both have an early dinner you can get up to your room before your Dad gets back from the pub."

Danny and I looked at each other with a nervous smile of relief. We didn't know why his car was at home and we didn't ask, we just wanted to eat and get up to our rooms as quickly as possible. All three of us sat down to have beans on toast. Dad spent all our money on drink so we never really had much more than beans or spaghetti on toast. If we were really lucky we'd have cereal for breakfast, but usually we just had a banana because Dad said cereals are far too expensive and a waste of money. Huh, waste of money – he's the waste of money, his drinking is a waste of money. But who are we? We're only kids, so what do we matter? I could tell Mum was nervous about Dad coming home as she rushed us through our dinner. We always knew when she was going to *get it* from him as she did everything very quickly just to get us out of the way.

We were just finishing our stodgy beans and soggy toast when we heard Dad's footsteps then the sound of him falling into the door. At the very same time all three of us gasped and panicked, jumping up from the table, still with food on our plates, Mum whispered, "Hurry up! Run, get up to your rooms."

We both ran so fast that we were huffing and puffing by the time we got to the top of the stairs as we ran into my bedroom. I always preferred to get Danny settled in his own room first so he felt safe, when I knew Dad was going to go off on one, but we didn't have time. We shut the door behind us and poor Danny sobbed his heart out. I hated living like this and I hated seeing what Dad was doing to us. I thought about Mirabriel, but to be honest I thought I'd imagined her, because I hadn't seen her since the night before. But it wouldn't hurt to have just one more look, would it? I gave Danny a hug and told him to do his homework and forget about what was going to happen downstairs.

As he went into his bag I looked under my bed again for the rainbow stars that Mirabriel had scattered. They just had to be there, somewhere, they *had* to be. I was so sure I hadn't imagined it. I searched frantically, pulling my bedcovers apart again to try and find them. I suddenly became aware that Danny was watching me.

"What on earth are you doing" he asked.

I didn't know how to tell him, he'd never believe me. Gee, I didn't know if I believed it myself right then!

"I think I've lost something" I lied. Well it wasn't really a lie because I had lost something, I just didn't know if what I'd lost really existed. Even when Danny asked me what I'd lost I still couldn't tell him. We froze as we heard smashing noises from downstairs. We could hear Mum screaming for Dad to stop whatever he was doing to her. Danny was crying inconsolably, saying he didn't want to live like this anymore.

Without thinking, I blurted out, "You don't need to. Mirabriel can help us, she told me last night."

"Eh?" he asked as his tears flowed. I sat quietly with only the sounds of smashing to be heard. *I'm stupid, I'm a fool.* I thought. What on earth had I been thinking saying that to Danny? Why had I opened my big mouth? Now, I was going to have to tell him that I'd been dreaming but he was already looking at me like I was crazy. How was I going to get out of this one?

"Dawn, tell me, *who* is going to help us? Who is Mirabriel? And where were you last night?" he asked.

"It's nothing Danny, I don't know what I'm talking about," I tried to fob him off and put my fingers inside my ears to block out the noise from downstairs.

"But you said…"

Just as Danny started to speak a bright flash appeared over my bed. I just knew it! I knew it, I knew it! My heart leapt with joy and I wanted to bounce around the room like Tigger in Winnie the Pooh.

CHAPTER THREE

I knew what was coming next.

"Mirabriel" I shouted before quickly putting my hand over my mouth, realising that I'd shouted it out aloud. But it was okay, they were still screaming at each other downstairs so they wouldn't have heard me anyway. I looked at Danny and his eyes were wide open, like he'd just seen a ghost! A burst of white appeared with lots of coloured stars falling all over my bed and the butterfly I'd seen the night before appeared in the middle of it.

"Danny, you can see her, can't you? Don't be scared, this is Mirabriel" I whispered as I hugged him tight. "She's here to help us."

Just at that moment Mirabriel flew from the middle of the air onto my bed. She was flapping her wings. "Danny, do not be afraid. I am indeed here to help you." She flew over Danny who jumped in fright and cuddled into me. I was a bit scared too, but I couldn't let Danny see that because in my heart I knew I could trust her.

"Children, do not fear, your Frangel Mirabriel is here, to do the best that she can do, to make your dreams and wishes come true." She flapped her wings three times and the Amitola burst into white light! All we could see was lots of coloured dust. I should have been scared, but something about Mirabriel made me feel so very calm and happy and told me not to be afraid. I looked at Danny and his eyes were wide open in amazement.

"Are you okay, Danny?" I asked as I put my arm around him.

"Y…y… yeeeeessssss," was his stuttered reply. "Dawn, I feel like I should be screaming for Mum, but I'm not afraid. Why am I not afraid? I don't even want Mum to know because it's making me forget what is going on." The sounds of screaming and smashing could still be heard downstairs. Danny looked at me for an answer, or maybe just reassurance that it was okay not to be afraid. "What's she going to do, Dawn?"

The smoke had cleared and all that could be seen was a bright white light, the brightest I'd ever seen.

"Sweet children, if you would like, I can show you how to block out all the noise from downstairs and take you somewhere that is so much fun that you'll forget what is going on. What do you say? Would you like to visit the World Of Light?" Mirabriel was smiling as she asked. In my heart I knew that I could trust her and apart from anything else, nothing could be worse than what was going on downstairs. So many times Danny and I talked about running away, just to escape, but we couldn't leave Mum. Dad could seriously hurt her one day and we needed to be here to help her. If only Mum would listen to her friend and escape, we could all get out of this horrible mess.

Danny and I looked at each other, a little unsure but also excited and at the same time we both nodded in agreement. Mirabriel looked happy as she flapped her wings once... twice...

"Stop!" I shouted. "What happens if Mum or Dad come up to our room and see you here?"

Mirabriel smiled. "Don't be afraid. They will never see me, I decide who sees me and I can disappear as quickly as I appear. We won't be here anyway, we are going to the World Of Light and I will make sure that you are back in your own beds if they come up the stairs."

"So, are you ready?" she asked in the softest, sweetest voice.

Once again she flapped her wings once... twice... three times...

"Wow! This place really is magical." I said as I grinned from ear to ear.

The colours were so bright that it looked as if someone had a volume control for the colour and they had turned it up full. I held Danny's hand. He was smiling so much I thought his wee face was going to burst. There were miles and miles of green grass and it was so beautiful and bright that I felt like I needed sunglasses. There was so much going on, I didn't know where to look first. There were rainbows everywhere – I didn't know you could get so many bright rainbows in one place! There were people - at least they kind of looked like people - running around and giggling, animals playing and birds singing. I could see trees, and huge rocks that looked like houses, and the biggest thing I noticed was that nobody was fighting, shouting or yelling. Everyone seemed so happy.

What was this place? It wasn't normal, not like we knew normal, anyway. The only thing I was sure of was that I loved it here already and I never ever wanted to go back home.

There was laughter everywhere and everyone was having so much fun. I watched them laughing and giggling - Mirabriel stood and smiled as she watched Danny and me look on in amazement.

"Run, children, run and have as much fun as you can find. Fear not, I will have you home in your beds before your Mum and Dad know you are away." With that she disappeared. I actually didn't care if Mum and Dad knew we were missing. *I'm never going home anyway,* I thought, *I'm staying here forever.* By the look on Danny's face I could tell he felt the same.

"Come on, Dawn!" Danny said as I heard his name being called. I looked around and saw a giant tree, smiling. Really? I rubbed my eyes, thinking I must have imagined it, when I heard a giggle and Danny's name being called again. I was sure it was the tree. It had the biggest, greenest eyes with little black dots in the middle and they were definitely looking at Danny. I didn't even know that trees could talk, I thought that was just in silly kids' TV programmes. Anyway how did it know his name? I was curious and excited at the same time and I could see Danny was just as excited. He ran towards it, calling for me to follow but he didn't even wait for me. He ran towards the tree so fast I thought he was going to fall over.

I was about to follow him when a very beautiful fairy appeared in front of me, I didn't think fairies were real, except in story books, but this was definitely real. She was so pretty, with kind green eyes that sparkled so brightly they lit up every time she moved. She had long red hair and spoke with a very gentle voice. She ran up to me excitedly. "Dawn, I am

so glad you're here! C'mon let's have some fun."
Before I had the chance to ask her how she knew my
name she'd grabbed my hand and started running. We
had run about three paces when I felt my feet leave the
ground. I couldn't feel the ground beneath my feet!
Was I flying? I looked down and we were going higher
and higher into the air. I was giggling so much and I
couldn't stop, I was so happy. I looked down at the
bright green grass. There was so much going on and
everyone was happy, I couldn't take it all in.

"Are you having fun?" the fairy who was
holding my hand shouted over. I could only nod. I
couldn't speak because I couldn't stop smiling.

"I am a Frangel and my name is Frangel
Briadh," she shouted over, making me giggle even
more.

"What is your name?" I asked unsure of what
she said.

"Frangel B....r.....i......a" she said very slowly "It
is spelt "BRIADH."

"Why do they call you that?" I asked between
giggles. She told me it was Garlic for beautiful.

"Garlic?" I screeched "Why on earth do you get
called garlic? Isn't that something you are meant to
eat?"

Frangel Briadh laughed so hard I thought we
were going to fall out of the sky.

"Gaelic, not garlic" she managed to say in
between giggles "Gaelic is the language they speak
where I come from in Scotland and Briadh means
beautiful in that language" she finished.

"Woah" I was mesmerised "Does that mean
you can speak another language?" I asked in awe.

"YES" she replied, though I had no idea what she said after it.

"Pardon" I asked, thinking my ears had not picked her up right.

"Chan eil aon chànan gu leòr" Frangel Briadh replied.

"Ah, you are speaking garlic again" I said excited and frustrated at the same time. "Please tell me what you are saying," I begged her.

"I said yes first, then when you said pardon I said one language is never enough" Frangel Briadh clarified "And its pronounced G..A...L...I...C ..... not garlic" she chuckled "Though it is spelled G-A-E-L-I-C" she clarified.

"Does everyone speak like that where you come from?" I asked her "It sounds like a lovely way to speak, would you take me to your friends and teach me, please?" I begged her.

"Yes, of course" Frangel Briadh replied.

"Where are you from? What do your friends look like? Do they look like you?" I asked her, wanting to know everything. "Oh, I'm sorry I didn't mean to sound nosey, It's just that I think you are beautiful, I love the way you speak and I'd love to learn more" I told her "I want to stay here forever and never go back home" I said sadly, yet happy at the same time. "Everyone seems so happy, there's no fighting" I said in the shocked and surprised manner in which I felt it.

"Dawn. You are right we don't fight here. We may not always agree with each other, but we wouldn't hurt each other. The only people you need to be careful of here are the Wartons, they are the only ones who do not like to see people happy. They love being miserable and want everyone else to be miserable too" she told me.

I was very surprised as I didn't think there would be anybody like that here in the World Of Light, it was such a happy place. Frangel Briadh must have heard my thoughts and very quickly warned me "You may not have seen them yet, but be warned they are out there."

I wanted to know more "How will I know them? What do they look like?" I quizzed.

Frangel Briadh told me that they were just like me and Danny – they looked just like "normal" people except they would look miserable. She told me that they found it very hard to be happy but she stressed that if they needed to look happy to trick someone, then they could by smiling and pretending that they were nice.

"You mean just like my Dad? He can do that too. He can be so horrible and mean to my Mum but sometimes if we walk downstairs he can pretend he is happy and nothing is wrong" I told her.

"That is exactly what I mean" she replied. "I may tell you more about the Wartons another time, but for now just be aware that they do not want the rainbow light to reach the earthly world as it is making too many people happy and they will do anything to destroy it. Now, let's go have some more fun" Frangel Briadh said as she pulled my arm "Are you ready?"

"For what?" I replied as I wondered what the rainbow light was. I'd never been this happy before, not ever.

"Ready to fly on your own?" she asked with a cheeky look on her face.

Aha. Now I was starting to see this Frangels mischievous side. I was about to ask her not to let go of me when she let go my hand and I started to panic in case I fell, but I knew I could trust Frangel Briadh so I tried to relax again and let myself have fun. She flew right in front of me laughing and asked, "Fall, why would you fall? You're flying. Here in World Of Light, you can do anything you like," and she flew a little distance away from me.

"C'mon, I want to show you my thistle house."

But I didn't follow her because I was having so much fun flying all by myself. Nor did I stop to ask her why she would live in a house made of jaggy thistles. I'd just discovered I could fly, so fly is what I was going to do! I started flying sideways then flipped over onto my tummy like those fast planes do, pretending I was one of them. I twisted round and round and felt the warm air on my face. I was having so much fun that I didn't see the seagull coming towards me. Bang!

"Oi! Dawn, when you're flying mind your poor feathered friends up here too, would ya?" the seagull said flying off squawking a happy song which I found myself singing too. "I'm free as a bird and I can fly, I'm as free as a bird and I love to try." Wow, he knew my name. Everyone knows my name! He was still happy and singing even though I flew into him. Why didn't he hit me or scream at me because it was my fault? Nobody seems to get angry here and I didn't really understand it, I thought to myself as I carried on flying, more carefully this time.

"Look at me, Dawn! Wahoooooo, I'm soooo happy!" Danny yelled as he flew past me on the back of a dinosaur! Was I dreaming? I nipped myself hard to see if I was awake and I fell to the ground with a thump. But as soon as I landed I was thrown back up, like a trampoline. Suddenly a fairy appeared out of the middle of the grass. She was so tiny, the size of a plum. She flew up and landed on top of my head, peering down into my eyes. Did I really have a plum-sized fairy on top of my head, talking to me whilst she was upside down?

"Yes you do," she said "And I'm not a fairy I'm a Frangel– we come in all shapes and sizes ya know."

"Wow! Did you just hear my thoughts? How do I know if you are an angel or a fairy or something else?" I asked. She giggled as she told me everyone, apart from the Wartons, in the World Of Light are Frangels before offering me some candy floss.

"Go on, have as much as you like," she said as she jumped off my head and started eating what looked like pink fluffy grass. I couldn't take the gorgeous sweet smell any longer and I started eating it too. Mmmmm, it really was candy floss grass. They'd never need to cut the grass here I thought. I'd cut it for them no problem. I ate so much candy that I felt sick. I could feel the sticky pink mess all over my face. But it was worth it, it was the best tasting candy floss I had ever eaten – but it had to be the best as I'd never had candy floss before. I'd seen it, but we weren't allowed treats like that at home. Soon, I'd had enough and wanted to find Frangel Briadh, I'd been having so much fun that I'd forgotten all about her. She'd be so angry with me for not doing as I was told. I panicked and thought I'd better fly back to find her.

I thanked the candy Frangel and started to run, expecting to take-off like I had earlier. But nothing happened. I ran again, faster, but still nothing happened. I ran again even faster this time and fell flat on my face. I heard giggling – there was a snail on the grass laughing at me.

"What are you laughing at?" I scolded, embarrassed by my feeble attempts to fly. I was half-angry he was laughing at me and half-surprised that a snail could laugh.

"You'll never fly with that cobweb on your hair," he told me.

"What do you mean?" I asked.

The snail, which was the size of a cat, said, "It looks like the candy Frangel has sprung onto your head, you have candy webs on your hair. They stop you from flying."

"So how do I get rid of it?" I asked as I felt the top of my head. I could feel a pile of stringy stuff but it wouldn't come off.

"You need to go to Frangel Briadh's house and ask her pet spiders to remove it." he informed me.

I couldn't stop giggling at the thought of a spider removing candy floss from my hair. I wonder if they eat it I thought, or maybe they had webs made of candy floss. I had no idea how to find Frangel Briadh's house. I remember her telling me it was a thistle house, but I didn't even know where I was. Not sure I can negotiate the stabbys on the outside of the house anyway I thought as I visualised a large thistle with a door.

Oh Frangel Briadh where are you and why did I not follow you like you told me to? Just as I was about to ask the snail he'd vanished. I didn't even know his name to call him back to help me. I felt a little frightened not knowing where I was but at that moment Frangel Briadh appeared out of nowhere. Just like Mirabriel always did.

"You called?" she giggled. I stood with my mouth wide open in shock that she too had heard my thoughts. "Close your mouth," Frangel Briadh said, "before you catch flies!" We both laughed.

"Why is it so happy here and why aren't you mad at me for not following you? I can't feel sad here, it's the happiest place I've ever been to in my whole life."

Frangel Briadh looked serious for once. "Dawn, you can be this happy all the time. When you're not here you just have to close your eyes and pretend that you are. Our brains are so clever and powerful that they can make us feel anything we want. We can choose to be happy or sad by choosing the thoughts we think. If you feel sad when you hear fighting or shouting at home and you try really hard to have happy thoughts and imagine that you're here, it will help you feel happier. It may not stop the fighting but it sure will help you cope better when you hear it" She was smiling and she seemed to understand how hard life was at home for Danny and me. Was she trying to help? Well, if she was she'd sure succeeded.

"Wait a minute, how do you know there's a lot of fighting at my house?" I asked, puzzled.

"Dawn, Dawn, Dawn. My dear child. I'm with you always. I see and hear everything - all you need to do is call me and I'll come to you. Now I've got someone special I'd like you to meet" she finished.

"Neigh, neigh you know what to do,
Gallop over here so we can sit on you."

With that Frangel Briadh snapped her fingers and two beautiful white horses appeared from nowhere. I've no idea how I got on it, but next minute we were sitting on one each. I was amazed – these were the most beautiful horses I'd ever seen. Frangel Briadh was next to me on a horse called 'Dreamer.' She told me that if I wanted to know the name of my horse all I had to do was to close my eyes and ask him and he'd tell me through my thoughts. I closed my eyes and asked. It took a few moments but I heard the name, 'Jeremiah.'

"Wow, it worked" I said excitedly. "My horse is called Jeremiah."

Frangel Briadh giggled. "Look at Jeremiah's head, Dawn. What do you see?"

I looked and saw his eyes and ears and... *Oh my goodness he had a horn in the middle of his head!*

"Is... is...? No it can't be," I stammered.

Frangel Briadh laughed. "Yes Dawn, it can be. Jeremiah and Dreamer are unicorns." Before I could say anything else we were floating through the air next to each other.

"But how do I...?" before I could finish I was in my bed with my nighty on and my light out. My Mum came into my room and asked if I was okay. I nodded but couldn't speak. I was a mixture of confused, happy and mad that I was back in this place. My Mum looked a mess and I could tell she had been crying but somehow it didn't affect me the way it normally would have. In fact, I couldn't wait for her to get out of my room so I could work out what was going on and get back to that magical place.

"Good night, I love you." With those words my Mum kissed my forehead and left the room. I was confused, yet happy and excited all at the same time. I was about to rub my eyes when Mirabriel jumped out from between my pillows.

"What... how...?" I couldn't get the words out. I heard Mirabriel giggling.

"My dear child, I told you to trust me to have you back in your bedroom before they noticed that you were missing."

"Where's Danny?" I panicked.

"He's in his bed, just as you are, Dawn. You have nothing to fear," Mirabriel said softly. I was so grateful we didn't get caught.

"Thank you Mirabriel, for letting me feel happy, I loved it so much," I said, with tears in my eyes realising that I was back to reality. I was sad it was over but I was still beaming from all that had happened in the World Of Light.

"Remember what your Frangel sister told you, she is by your side always, just as I am. All you need to do is think about us or call our names and we will be right there with you. Good night, dear child, you must rest now." Before I had the chance to say anything else there was the familiar bright light and waterfall of stars forming a perfect rainbow before she melted into it and disappeared.

Frangel sister, wow I have a sister. Wopppeee! I thought, I'd always wanted a sister, I mean I love Danny of course, but he's my brother, and brothers are annoying. I wondered who my Frangel sister was. Ooohhhh it must be Frangel Briadh - she was the only other one who'd told me she was there for me. I was so excited that I couldn't close my eyes. I wanted to speak to Danny but I could hear Mum speaking to him in his room. At least I knew he was back safe. I'd not have been best pleased if he'd got to stay in World Of Light and I didn't.

CHAPTER FOUR

I must have fallen asleep very quickly as I woke to the bright sun coming through my bedroom curtains. For the first time ever I could hear the birds singing, which is something I'd never noticed before. I lay in bed and giggled as I remembered the poor bird I crashed into when I was flying!

I went downstairs for breakfast to find Danny eating a banana, with a huge smile spread right across his face. We were both giggling as Mum came into the kitchen, looking her usual mess.

"What's so funny?" she demanded in a grumpy voice.

"N... n... nothing" Danny said as I shot him a look to warn him to not say anything. Next minute, without warning, Danny burst out "Mum, Mum I was flying with a dinosaur last night!"

I couldn't believe Danny was about to blow our secret. The only time in my life I ever remembered feeling happy, truly happy, it was like my heart was singing and my feet were bouncing and he was about to blow it all. Spoil sport, just like the annoying little brother that he could be. I was about to say something when Mum spoke first, "Danny stop talking nonsense and finish your breakfast before you're late for school" and she turned her back.

I quickly booted him in the leg before he could say anything else.

"Ouch!" he yelped.

"Danny what's going on with you today? I've told you already to get a move on and stop that stupid screeching," Mum yelled at him. Danny saw my face and knew from Mum's reaction that this was not the time. He apologised in a quiet, quivering voice telling Mum he'd hit his leg off the table. I grabbed him by his collar and said we had to go or we'd be late. I wanted to get him out of there as fast as I could. Mum disappeared back to her bed as we left.

As soon as we got outside Danny asked, "What was that for?"

"Danny, did you have fun last night?" I asked.

"Yes" he replied quickly.

"Were you happy?"

"Oooohhhh, yes I sure was that!" Danny exclaimed.

"Okay, tell me the last time you felt that happy" I asked. He paused as we started walking to school. He was silent for what seemed like ages until he eventually said, in a sad voice, "Dawn, I don't think I've ever been happy and if I have then I don't remember it. I've never been that happy in my life, not ever."

"Right!" I said. "Then you do not tell anybody what happened last night – not a single person, not even your school friends. If you do, they will think that we're either mad or they'll try and spoil your fun by stopping it. Do you understand?" I think I was more worried about me losing out than him.

"Dawn, I don't want anyone to spoil it, I want to go and live there forever. I want to go there and never come back." he said with tears in his eyes. His tears didn't last long as he started laughing, telling me how he'd flown with a dinosaur, had a sword fight with a toy soldier, eaten bubble gum which was growing from a tree, raced a snail (and lost) and had been shown how to do magic tricks by a gnome.

"Wow, Danny, you had as much fun as I did," I said before continuing my lecture, "That is why you mustn't tell anybody. We don't want to lose it, okay? Got it?"

"Pinkie promise I won't tell," he said and we shook our pinkie fingers together as we continued to chat excitedly about our adventures the night before. We chatted all the way to school. Just as we were nearly there Danny asked how to get back to the World Of Light. I told him what Mirabriel had said about just having to call her name or think about her and she'd be there.

"Ah wait a minute" I said out loud......let me try something" I said as I tried really hard to think of Mirabriel. I'm sure this is what I did once before and just as I had Mirabriel appeared.

Danny shouted out so loud that a few people turned to look at him "Mirabriel."

I quickly put my hand over his mouth to stop him but it was too late, Mirabriel appeared in a bright burst of light. She hovered above the middle of the pavement.

I panicked, "Mirabriel, you must leave, you must go quickly before someone sees you!"

"Don't fret, nobody apart from you and Danny can see me," Mirabriel tried to reassure me. I looked at everyone around us and it was true – nobody saw her, even though she came in the brightest flash of light with her wings spread wide in the middle of the air. Wow, this really was cool.

"Run, you pair, before you are late for school." And with that Mirabriel disappeared in the middle of a bright rainbow that nobody else seemed to notice. Danny and I both looked around at the same time to see if anybody had seen it, but they hadn't.

"Hi Dan!" shouted Mark who had walked up to Danny from behind. The rainbow stars were still falling but Mark clearly didn't see them. So then we knew for sure that nobody else could see our special friend. I smiled so much I thought my mouth was going to rip. I felt special, lucky and so very happy. And I could tell that Danny did too. We'd skipped into school feeling more happiness than we'd ever known.

That day at school was a day we'd been waiting for all week. Everyone in the whole school was going to take part in a competition to spend a week at the local zoo helping the keepers look after the animals. It wouldn't be difficult, I'd thought, as all we had to do was spot the differences between two pictures then write why we wanted to win the competition.

After lunchtime the upper years of the school arrived in the hall, which was prepared with lots of desks and chairs. I sat near the back because I hated being in the middle where people could see me. I saw Danny sit down at the front. I hoped he'd win because he wanted it so much. He loves animals and had been excited about this since he'd heard about it. Dad wouldn't let us have any pets, which is really sad because Danny has a very special bond with animals. It would make him so happy and at the same time it would get him away from the fighting at home. Even though he could be annoying I really wanted to see him happy and smiling. Danny came into the hall and clocked me, he gave me the thumbs up as if to say, *I'm going to win.* I smiled at him and shook my head laughing.

After the teacher gave us the talk about what we had to do and how we weren't allowed to chat, we all started. We were told we had one hour to complete the competition. When I'd finished writing I went back to spotting the difference between the two pictures as they were really hard. I'd thought it was going to be easy, but it wasn't.

I only had one left to find when the teacher shouted, "Last ten minutes."

I looked towards Danny to find him looking a bit flustered. He was fidgeting a lot and kept hitting his pencil off his leg. I hoped he'd managed to finish it as I knew how upset he'd be if he didn't. I found the last difference and put my pencil down. I sat back and looked towards Danny. He had his head in his hands. All of a sudden I saw Mirabriel – she'd appeared in front of Danny in her usual shower of stars and was hovering above his desk. I saw his head shoot up so fast I was surprised it didn't fall off! I panicked, looking around the hall, but nobody seemed to notice Mirabriel, or Danny, not even the teachers. Huh, shows how special Danny is when he was the only one who could see her – and me too of course! I realised how special we must be. Just a pity Mum and Dad didn't think so too. I wondered what Mirabriel was saying to Danny.

"Dawn, never mind what I'm saying to Danny, and yes before you ask, I can hear your thoughts too," she chuckled.

Wow! I thought again, *this just keeps getting better and better.* I hoped nobody else could hear her.

"No, Dawn, just you and Danny," Mirabriel giggled.

I couldn't hear what she was saying to Danny but he was scribbling like mad on his paper. *He's such a cheat,* I thought, *I can't believe he is getting the answers from Mirabriel.* I knew how much he wanted it but it made me mad to think he was cheating because that was just wrong!

All of a sudden a huge rainbow appeared between Danny and I which Mirabriel slid over, landing on the desk in front of me.

"Now, Dawn, Danny certainly did not cheat. Cheating gets you nowhere. If you really want something all you need to do is believe you can achieve it and you will. If you believe you can finish the competition, then you will. Cheating is not necessary. If you don't manage to do it then you must trust and believe there is a very good reason that you are not meant to finish it. Sometimes things happen and we think the world is against us but there is almost always a reason, and it's almost always for the best, you just don't always see that reason at the time. Sometimes it takes months or years to understand. But you must learn to trust in yourself and know most things in life teach us valuable lessons that can help us as we grow older." And with that, Mirabriel disappeared.

The teacher shouted, "Time's up, put your pencils down."

Danny looked up at me and smiled with his thumbs up. Even though I thought he was cheating I still hoped he'd win. I guessed that there were so many people who had entered that I doubted he would win.

As I was pondering this, Mirabriel appeared again. "Dawn, if you think you won't win and you expect to fail, then guess what will happen? You will fail. Choose your thoughts wisely, dear child. Almost every negative thought has a positive thought – you just have to look hard enough to find it" and off she went again. I didn't know what to think. I was frightened to think anything now as I knew Mirabriel could hear all of my thoughts. We handed in our papers and went back to class.

After school I met Danny at the bus stop, as I always did. He couldn't stop smiling. There was nobody else at the bus stop and the first thing I said to Danny was, "What are you smiling like that for, did you cheat?"

He looked upset "No, I did not!"

I felt bad that I'd doubted him and explained that I'd seen him struggling until Mirabriel appeared. He started smiling again and got excited as he told me that he'd finished the 'spot the difference' but he'd been stuck as he could only think of one reason why he should win and that was because he loved animals. He knew the teacher told us that to win our reason would really have to stand out from the rest, and he couldn't think of anything. He told me that he thought to himself that if Mirabriel was there she'd know what to write and at that very thought she appeared. He'd begged her to tell him what to write but all she told him was that he had to believe in himself first. He had to feel in his heart and in his tummy that he was the person that most deserved to win and if he really truly believed that then he would know what to write. She'd asked him why he thought he should win over anybody else and she disappeared.

"Dawn, I had no idea what my reasons were but when she left I did exactly what she told me and let myself believe that I really was the best person and I just couldn't stop writing. So many thoughts came to me that my hand couldn't keep up with them!" Danny was so excited as he was telling me that he was nearly shouting as he said "Dawn, I AM the best person to work with those animals. I just know I am."

I put my arm around his shoulder and gave him the biggest, big sister hug - it made me so happy to see him so happy. Yes, he could be annoying and sometimes I fell out with him, but I never forgot how sad he could be too. He's sad more often than he is annoying or happy. I guess we both are.

We got off the bus and skipped towards the house. Yet again, at exactly the same time we both held our breath and our skip changed to a slow walking pace. The closer we got to home, the further our happiness moved away from us. It was amazing just how much we both felt the same thing at the same time without thinking or saying anything. Just the sight of home took us back to real life once again.

CHAPTER FIVE

"Come on Dan, let's not let anything spoil our happiness. Just for once let's walk in the door happy." I gave him another one of my special big sister hugs. Danny threw my arm off his shoulder, "Yuk! Will you stop doing that, my friends might see you," he protested.

Trying to take his mind off home I got him talking about the animals at the zoo. He got so carried away that he didn't realise that he was home until we walked in the door. Mum seemed to be in a good mood until Danny told her about the competition, she seemed very unhappy about it and we both noticed the change in her straight away.

"Why can't you be happy for me?" Danny cried as Mum became agitated whilst trying to persuade Danny that she was happy for him.

"No! No! You are not!" he shouted at her.

"Danny, I am happy for you, and nothing would make me happier than to know you were happy but I'm worried about what your Dad will say if you do win."

"Mum, when are you going to get us out of here?" Danny screamed at her. "You're always saying you can't, but if you really wanted to you would believe that you could do it and ask those people, Women whatever they are called, to help us. I know you are afraid but I also know your friend told you that those people could help us get out of here. If you really wanted to then you would believe it was possible and do something about it, so you obviously don't want to!" He ran up to his room.

Mum looked at me, asking what his outburst was about and what we knew about the conversation between her and her friend. I told her how much he really wanted to win the competition but not before I admitted that I had been listening into her conversation. I asked her if it was true and if she knew what Women's Aid was. I thought I was going to be in trouble but she never told me off. She just told me that she knew Women's Aid were there to help people in situations like ours and her friend wanted to put her in touch with one of the ladies who worked there, but she refused because she couldn't risk Dad finding out. It didn't matter what I said, she was clearly never going to change her mind.

"Would you just leave it Dawn, go upstairs before your Dad gets home."

Danny was lying on his bed crying. "Dawn, if I win I'm going, I don't care what that monster says about it. No…no, hold on…..WHEN I win I WILL be going" he said with real conviction.

"Danny you mustn't ever tell Mum or Dad or anybody about our Frangel, do you hear me?" I pleaded with him.

"Dawn, Frangel Mirabriel is just stupid! Anyway she's not my Frangel, she's your Frangel. Frangels with skirts are for sissies," Danny replied. I was shocked as I'd never heard him speak negatively of Mirabriel, she had helped us feel so much better when she was around.

"What do you mean, Danny? You saw her with your own eyes, you aren't making any sense," I said.

"I know I did, but I don't want your Frangel, I want my own Frangel and if I had one I'd call him my night warrior!" He stood on top of his bed and pointed both his arms in the air as he shouted "Night Warrior!"

"Hello, Danny my friend, you called?" Danny looked surprised as what he saw was not the beautiful butterfly we knew to be Mirabriel. I jumped in fright at the creature in front of us. Was it Mirabriel? The room felt calm like it did when she appeared but she looked so different.

This was more than just an Eagle I thought to myself. I can't explain what I felt other than it was a very wise bird and his eyes spoke to me. His eyes were very large and round and when I looked in them I thought at first they were brown then I looked in them again and they looked green. I don't know if they changed or if I was just not seeing them properly. He had large shoulders, which I guess were his wings all hunched up. When he first appeared his wings were wide open like huge fans made of brown and white feathers. He had a big beak which was shaped like a crooked finger, golden in colour and when he spoke his beak opened to show a pink tongue as he spoke with a soft and gentle voice, just like Mirabriel. I was so confused and although I'd initially felt scared, it didn't last long as I soon felt the safe peaceful feeling I had when Mirabriel was around.

"I am your Eagle Warrior of Light Danny, your very own Frangel, I will also answer to Night Warrior as you like to call me" came the voice "all you need to do is think about me and I'll be here. When you shouted 'Night Warrior' you pictured me in your mind, which allowed me to know for sure that you wanted me to appear, so here I am. I can come in any form you wish. If you think of me in your mind's eye as a warrior, then that is how I shall appear. Frangels can appear in lots of different ways and everyone has one of their own" he reassured him.

Danny was stuck for words, which didn't happen very often. He also looked a bit embarrassed. "I'm......erm... I hope you don't mind if I call you a Night Warrior" he said in a shaky voice. "You look so much better as an eagle than a butterfly" he finished.

The Eagle Warrior of Light chuckled and said, "No, of course not. You can call me anything you like, as long as it is polite." Danny looked relieved.

"Does that mean you can go to the World Of Light too Eagle Warrior of Light?" Danny asked excitedly.

"Oh yes, I certainly can"

"Oh, please, can you take us there? I'd love to go there with you. Please?"

"Danny…"

Before he could finish what he was saying he disappeared and Mum walked into Danny's room. We jumped as she came in the door, and we must have looked startled, because she immediately asked what we were up to.

"I just got a fright, Mum as I didn't hear you come up the stairs," I tried to convince her. "I was just trying to cheer Danny up and tell him not to worry about the competition."

I always knew when she was dreading Dad coming home. She'd be agitated, knowing what kind of mood he was likely to be in, and she was usually right.

"Danny. I'd love you to win the competition, but please don't say anything in front of your Dad tonight, okay?" she pleaded.

"No Mum, that's just not fair, why should I miss out just 'cos he doesn't like it? I hate him and I wish he'd disappear. You say he just needs help, but he will never get help, so he won't ever change. Now please just get out of my room and leave me alone. I'll probably not win anyway so you can be happy. Now GET OUT!" he screeched.

It was so unlike him, usually Danny was quiet and just got on with everything. He was really unhappy and it wounded me to see him like that, and it also made me sad to see Mum looking so upset as she left the room.

As soon as Mum left, before I had a chance to say anything to Danny, the Eagle Warrior of Light appeared "Now Danny, listen here, I know you are upset but you must never, ever believe you can't or won't achieve anything. Let me tell you something that many people just don't know."

"Do you know what a photocopier is Danny?" he continued.

Danny looked a combination of upset, angry and curious as he nodded.

"Well, Danny, our world is just like a giant photocopier and whatever you think about or say is photocopied and sent straight back to you."

Eagle Warrior of Light went on to explain that whatever Danny chose to think or believe, was what he would get back in life.

Looking a bit puzzled Danny asked, "So if I think I won't win then I won't win, is that what you mean?"

"Yes, that is exactly what I mean."

"So, if I think I'll win then I will win? So if everyone thinks they will win then they will - but we can't all win!" he exclaimed.

"Ah, smart young man, you have a very good point. But it's a little more complicated than that. Let me try to explain."

"We are all made up of energy. Our bodies are like a shell, their only use is to allow humans to live on earth, just as you do. But what is inside of you is energy. It's energy that makes the brain and the body work. You can't see it but it's there. Are you following me so far?" Eagle Warrior of Light looked at both of us and we nodded.

Danny looked confused and asked, "If I can't see it how do I know it's there?"

"Another good question. Let me ask you something. When you switch on your TV, do you see what makes it work?"

Danny nodded, "Yes, it's the button on the TV."

"So, what makes the button work?" he asked.

"Well, obviously the plug. If you don't plug it in it won't work," Danny replied.

"Very good Danny, you're right. But what makes the plug work?"

"Errmm… electricity?"

"Exactly! Electricity. Electrical energy. Now tell me, do you see the electricity?"

"Aahhh, no, but I know it's there. Okay now I get it," Danny responded excitedly.

The Eagle Warrior of Light wrapped his wings around Danny's head as lots of brightly coloured rainbow stars fell on his hair and down his face. Danny and I both giggled. "Wow you really are a Frangel like Mirabriel" Danny exclaimed.

"You've got it, now you understand that the electrical energy that makes your TV work is invisible, but you know it's there, so you can see there is no difference from human energy, just because you can't see it doesn't mean it's not there." The Eagle Warrior of Light looked happy that we were able to follow what he was telling us. We understood.

"So now you can see that our bodies are made up of energy just like the wire leading to the TV. So if you want to win this competition then you need to make your energy the same as all the others who want to win too by believing that you can also win" he explained further. "Danny, if you want to watch a children's TV programme, you wouldn't see it if you switched on the sports channel, would you?"

Danny shook his head.

"So if you don't believe you can win it's like being on the wrong channel, your energy is in the wrong place. Do you see?"

Danny nodded his head as he tried to take it all in. It was quite hard to get our heads around and totally understand.

"So is that like me giving up without even trying even though I've put all the work into the answers in the competition?" Danny asked.

The Eagle Warrior of Light nodded excitedly, happy that he understood.

"Well I ain't giving up. Uuuh-uhhhh, no way!" he shouted with his arms folded. "No way, I AM going to win that competition. I WILL be going to the zoo!" He shouted so loud that the Eagle Warrior of Light covered his ears with his wings and giggled.

It was one of the funniest things ever to see such a striking giant eagle speak like a human, even funnier than seeing a butterfly speak.

"I get it too," I whispered, and I believed that one day we would get out of this rotten home where Dad controlled us all and made us so miserable.

I looked to my right to see Mirabriel on my shoulder nodding too as she looked at me and whispered "he's right you know and my sweet, sweet Dawn you will indeed get out of the situation you are in my dear child, so keep believing. Sometimes things happen for reasons that we may not understand for quite some time."

"Would you like me to tell you a story that will explain what I mean?" Mirabriel asked.

I nodded wanting to hear more as I noticed Danny did too as his Eagle Warrior of Light disappeared the same way Mirabriel did when she went, with coloured stars floating up to form a rainbow which he melted into before it disappeared.

"Okay. Well, there were two Frangels who went away together on their holidays. On their way they stayed with different people. One day they stayed with a very rich family who let them stay in their house but they wouldn't give them a bed and made them sleep in a freezing cold basement. When they were there one of the Frangels noticed a hole in the wall so she repaired it for them.

"The next night the Frangels stayed with a very poor family who didn't have much, but they gave up their bed for the Frangels to sleep in whilst the couple slept in the basement. In the morning the Frangels woke up to hear the family upset and crying. The man of the house told the Frangels that their only cow had died overnight and now they had no milk to drink or feed the family with. When the Frangels left that house one Frangel said to the other that she was very angry and upset with her. She told her she couldn't understand why she'd helped the family who were rich but horrible, but for the family who were so poor yet so kind she did nothing and let their only cow die.

The Frangel replied to her that when they stayed in the basement of the rich house she'd noticed that the hole in the wall was full of gold so she filled it in so they couldn't find it. She went on to say that the family who had lost their cow – well, that night the Frangels came to take the man's wife to heaven, so instead she gave them the family's cow.

"So you see, things are not always what they seem and while something may look unfair or difficult there is often a very good reason for that. That is why you must learn to trust in the world and trust in your Frangels."

Danny laughed "I always thought Frangels were just in fairy tales."

"Oh, Danny, you have much to learn. I will say no more about Frangels for now but I hope that you can now see that we all have our very own guardian Frangel that never leaves us and is there to protect us."

Mirabriel smiled. "All you need to do is sit in silence, believe and talk to them, they are always there to help you, I hope I have helped you see that now."

"You have helped us so much" Dawn said, "Please tell us how to get back to World Of Light, Mirabriel, I love it there so much I want to go back and stay forever."

Mirabriel smiled and before she disappeared she promised that one day she would teach us how to get there on our own.

CHAPTER SIX

I felt like I had known the World Of Light all of my life, I loved it, it was such a happy place and it felt like home. I saw Jeremiah in the distance and made my way over to surprise him, but I'd only been walking for a few seconds when he suddenly appeared in front of me.

"Jeremiah" I said excitedly "I was just coming to see you" I told him as I wrapped my arms around his neck. Jeremiah didn't communicate in the way we do in the earthly world, instead we spoke to each other through our thoughts and feelings. Sometimes he would show me images in my head. We worked so well together through these thoughts and images that no words were needed.

"I missed you Jeremiah, I'm so happy to see you."

As Jeremiah looked into my eyes lots of images ran through my head, as if I was watching a movie. He showed me images of us flying over the World Of Light with lots of different little towns below us. He kept showing me a rainbow and I knew he wanted to take me to see it as he got down on his front two legs and I climbed onto his back, he was always very gentle with me. We lifted up into the air with such grace that I felt like I was part of Jeremiah. He told me that this is what it felt like to be at "one" with something – to feel as if you are part of it. I liked that feeling, a lot. It made me feel very peaceful inside. This time Jeremiah told me he was going to show me more of the World Of Light. I thought I'd seen it all until I saw lots of different places below me. Jeremiah told me they were like lots of different kingdoms in the World Of Light, which were called pods. He told me the Light Pod was the place that was trying to make the earthly world a better place. It was the place where the rainbows were under close protection.

Jeremiah flew me over the Animal pod where I saw many animals including huge elephants, oh how I'd love to ride on those one day.

Then you will Dawn, if you just see yourself doing it. Jeremiah expressed.

Ah, that's what Mirabriel told us I thought to myself.

As we continued flying I began feeling peaceful and happy in a way that I couldn't explain. Those feelings kept getting stronger and stronger. I looked up to see what was making me feel this way. All I could see were the clouds, until Jeremiah told me to look down. Beneath us was what Jeremiah described as the Light pod. I was about to ask Jeremiah why it was called the light pod when I saw the biggest, brightest rainbow. I had no idea that rainbows could be so perfect and so bright. Apart from the rainbow Mirabriel always disappeared in, most of the rainbows I'd seen were faded so only a little bit of it was visible and as you got closer to them they always seemed to get further away. Instead this one was whole and got bigger and brighter the closer we got. Before I could say anything to Jeremiah we were in the middle of the rainbow. It was as if I had glasses on with red lenses. It wasn't scary or anything like that. No, not scary at all – it was quite the opposite. In fact, it was definitely a very peaceful feeling.

As we reached the centre of the red in the rainbow, Mirabriel appeared on the top of Jeremiah's horn.

"Mirabriel, Mirabriel, this is so much fun and everything looks red, even you" I giggled.

Mirabriel chuckled "Dawn you are in the red zone of the rainbow in the World Of Light. This is a very special place to be."

"I feel everywhere in the World Of Light is special" I replied feeling very privileged to be here. "Mirabriel, this ...." I couldn't finish, all I could do was lift my jaw up as it fell wide open, unable to believe what I was seeing. I wasn't sure if I'd fallen off Jeremiah or if I was still flying…. but wait a minute…. I can't have because Mirabriel was still in the same position as if she was sitting on Jeremiah's horn and I was still on the same sitting position as if I was on his back. It felt like I was still there, but Jeremiah had disappeared. He had just vanished with no warning and he never said anything to me, he just vanished. I was deep in thought, trying to work out what was going on, waiting to fall from a great height, when I was taken out of my thoughts by the sound of Mirabriel laughing and Jeremiah reappearing.

"What........how............wh….?" I couldn't find the words.

"Dawn, my dearest sweet child, Jeremiah never left us, we were both still with him every bit as much as he was still with us, he just became invisible for a short time" Mirabriel enlightened me.

Jeremiah turned to look at me to confirm what Mirabriel had just told me and I heard his laughter as he did.

"Invisible? What do you mean invisible?" I asked.

"It means you can't see him, but he is still there" Mirabriel informed me.

"Yes, yes, I know what invisible means" I said irritably. I was so taken aback by what I saw....... or didn't see......that I couldn't express myself.

"I know Dawn, I was just teasing, let me explain what happened."

Mirabriel went on to explain that the World Of Light was made up of lots of special pods which all had different names. There was the Safari pod, the Pet pod, Gnome pod, Candyfloss pod and many more. She explained that each pod was like a small kingdom, each of which had something to teach us. She said everything in life was like that – no matter what experience we had in life it taught us something about ourselves or the world, but sometimes the experience could be so hard that we wouldn't always see what it taught us until after we had been through the experience.

"So, what is this pod called then?" I asked curiously, aware that we were going into a new pod.

"This is the Light pod, a very special pod indeed" Mirabriel informed me "This is where the rainbow light shines down onto the earthly world to help people heal and live a happier life. The rainbow light is the magic of the Light pod" she continued.

Mirabriel described the World Of Light as having so much love and happiness that they wanted everyone, everywhere, to have a share so they too could experience it. They wanted it to reach as many people as possible in the earthly world and by beaming down the magical colours of the rainbow that's exactly what it did.

I think I understood what she meant, kind of.

"You don't need to fully understand right now, it will all become clear in time, sweet child" Mirabriel informed me with a smile. "The only thing you need to be careful of here, in the World Of Light, are the Wartons. They live in the Warton pod and don't like people being happy.

They thrive on being miserable and want everyone else to be miserable too. For this reason, they are a threat to the Light pod because they are determined to get to the magical rainbow and shut it down to stop the rainbow light reaching earth and helping others.

You can help us protect the rainbow but for now let's go and show you around this magical place. I think you'll love it" Mirabriel finished.

Jeremiah let out a huge "neigh" in agreement. We glided down the rainbow, one stripe at a time, each one tainting the world through its own magical colour. I loved indigo the best. The world looked awesome when it was all purple. As we were coming out of the last colour of the rainbow I could see what looked like some sort of paradise below us. The sort of magical place you see in your happiest of dreams. There was a beautiful big pond with lots of rainbow coloured lights all around it. It looked as if it was beaming a light show of coloured sabres in a circle above us as we rode over the top. It felt very peaceful, as if I was having the nicest of dreams. Jeremiah flew over the Light pod to let me see the whole pod from above.

I heard lots of different sounds – peaceful sounds. Mirabriel had flown away after we left the rainbow and I saw her in the area next to the pond with the bright colours. The pond was surrounded by lots of busy things – I had no idea if they were people, animals, Frangels or what they were but I do know they all seemed to care for each other as they were friendly and even though they were busy they still seemed to have time to help each other out. There were trees everywhere.

I saw Lizards and other animals but I was confused as one of the lizards looked as if it kept changing. I kept watching one in particular, as he ran across the grass he suddenly stopped still and turned into a stone. I'm sure that's what I saw, no it couldn't have been, surely it wasn't possible I thought to myself! I kept watching the lizard...or stone.... or whatever it was and I saw a white light around it. I then saw a rabbit running around very fast, as if it was trying to scuttle away from something. It was a huge white rabbit, which was so big that I actually thought it was a cat at first. It ran for a few minutes until it also stopped and turned to stone. Now there was no doubting what I saw.

Mirabriel appeared from nowhere, as she does, and she fluttered around my head as she giggled telling me that all would soon become clear to me.

Jeremiah was now flying very low over the light pod. I'd lost count of how many rainbows we flew under and through. This place was magical. Everything was so bright and vibrant – the flowers, the animals, the grass, even the water was bright and looked alive.

I saw the rocks that the rabbit and lizard had turned into and as we got closer I watched them turn back into the animal that they originated from. They continued to run around and I could see they still had a kind of bright light around them, as if someone was shining a torch from above them. I wouldn't call the Light pod as much fun as some of the other pods in the World Of Light but it was definitely the pod that made me feel the happiest and at most peace, so far. There was just something extra special about it.

Jeremiah lowered himself further and I was excited to know that we were going to be stopping here. Just as his hooves hit the ground lots of pearlescent stars rose from his feet and two robins appeared, one on either side of me. They both had one end of a rainbow each in their beaks. They fluttered over me as Jeremiah told me it was ok to get off him, but before I had a chance to climb down I felt myself floating up above Jeremiah. The two robins still had the rainbow held over my head and as I moved so did the rainbow. The rainbow was acting like some sort of magnet moving me with it towards the bright coloured pond which Jeremiah called the enchanted water. He told me that sometimes the Wartons would succeed in hurting one of the light workers and this is where they took them to bathe and heal again. It is also the place that transforms anyone who wishes to become beautiful again.

"What do you mean become beautiful again? I don't understand. Does it make you pretty?" I asked.

"No, no, no, good gracious no. Being pretty does not make you beautiful. Beauty is on the inside my sweet child. You could be the prettiest girl or most handsome boy in the world, but if you are not nice to other people, if you only think of yourself or are nasty towards other people then it doesn't make you beautiful. Being beautiful is being kind to others, thinking of others, being honest, helping others and wanting them to feel nice instead of bad about themselves. That makes you a beautiful person.

It does not matter how old you are, whether you are a boy or a girl, how fat or thin you are. It does not matter what colour your skin is, what your religious beliefs are or where about in the world you live. We are all human beings. Being beautiful is recognising that and treating everyone with the same love and respect. When you look at the earth from space you do not see anything dividing the world, apart water, so nobody should be treated different just because they come from another part of the world. We all choose to travel different paths in life, but that does not make any one human being better than another, instead it gives us all different experiences of life, which lets us learn from one another. Being able to recognise that makes you beautiful.

We are all born beautiful but sadly some become unpleasant by being horrible to others, he said looking sad.

"But I don't understand why anybody would want to hurt someone else or make them feel bad about themselves. My Dad does it to my Mum all the time and I don't understand why" I said sadly as the reality of my life at home hit me.

Jeremiah nuzzled his head into me and I placed my arms around his neck and cried. That was the first time I felt sad in the World Of Light. Jeremiah told me that when somebody behaves in a nasty or unkind, thoughtless way it is usually because of something going on within that person and rather than feel those horrible feelings that makes them feel that way they try to make someone else feel them instead.

"So are you telling me that when my Dad is being horrible to my Mum it's not because she is a bad wife or Mum, like he tells her, but because he feels bad inside himself and rather than feel it he makes Mum think she is a bad person so she feels the horrible feelings instead?" I asked Jeremiah with my arms still wrapped around his neck.

"That's exactly what I mean" he confirmed. "And not just your Dad, but it's the same for bullies and anybody who tries to make someone feel bad about themselves" he finished.

"So, my Mum's not really a bad person then?" I asked crying a little harder as I realised the truth.

"No, Dawn, she's not. I'm not saying she doesn't have her faults, we all do, and nobody is perfect. But ask yourself does your Mum give you love? Make you feel nice about yourself? Does she love you or does she make you feel bad about yourself?" he asked

I didn't even need to take time to think of the answer. "My Mum loves me and shows me all the time. She tries to keep me safe as best as she can, she cuddles me and tells me she loves me. She always tells me nice things about who I am" I said smiling as I felt a nice warm glow thinking of just how much my Mum really did love me. "She can be very grumpy though and she can shout at me and Danny sometimes. Actually a lot" I finished.

Jeremiah nudged me off his neck and lowered his head to look into my eyes as he told me that the love my Mum shows me is her beauty inside and when she is angry or shouting that is because SHE is upset inside and doesn't really know how to cope with the bad way my Dad makes her feel. He also said that she didn't know how to cope with the bad way me and Danny are made to feel and because of all that she hurts inside. He said it didn't make it ok for her to shout but it did help explain some of the reasons for her doing it.

I guess it made sense, even if it was hard to believe or really understand.

"Thank you for explaining that Jeremiah" I said giving him another hug. His hugs made me feel all tingly, as if someone was blasting me with a dose of happiness.

"Would you like to experience the enchanted water?" Jeremiah asked me.

I was stunned, I didn't know what to say. Of course I'd love to but that water is for special people I thought to myself. I couldn't possibly use it. But then I realised that if Jeremiah was telling me to use the water that it must mean that I was not beautiful inside.

Jeremiah stopped my thoughts very quickly telling me that it's not just used to make people beautiful inside but it can also be used by anyone who was feeling bad inside. If they felt sad or negative it would turn all those unhappy feelings into the light making them feel beautiful again.

"What does negative mean?" I asked

"That is when you can only see the bad side of something. Almost every negative thought has a positive, but you need to look really hard to see it sometimes. And sometimes people are in such a sad or difficult situation that they can't see it no matter how hard they look. Think of it this way, if it rains outside many people can only think of how miserable it is and that they can't do anything because it's raining. But if only they could see that the rain is what waters the flowers to help them grow giving us such beautiful colours in our world. It makes the grass grow for us to play on, and it's what allows us to turn on a tap to drink a glass of water or flush the toilet. So, you see my sweet child, when you are soaking wet, freezing cold and your birthday party has been cancelled because it's raining the positive can be hard to see, but if you get into the habit of looking for the positive in every situation you WILL find something." Jeremiah explained.

I smiled at him, and then threw my arms around his neck, telling him I loved him. I really did understand and I trusted Jeremiah completely.

"Well, my happy one would you like to use the enchanted water to lift that little bit of sadness and let yourself be filled with love and happiness?" Jeremiah asked me

"Well, of course I'd love to, but isn't it just for special people?"

Jeremiah nudged me "Oi, you are special, so come on let's go, you will love it, I know you will."

Frangel Briadh suddenly appeared and challenged me to a race to the water.

I started to run in the direction of the water but I was suddenly confronted by a black iron gate covered in Ivy and I could no longer see the water, or Jeremiah.

I looked behind me, in front of me again and to each side but couldn't see her until I heard Frangel

Briadh laughing and I saw her peering through the ivy on the other side of the iron gate.

"Eh? What? How on earth did you manage to get through there, I never saw you open the gate?" I asked full of wonder and confusion.

"Ahhh you have much to learn my sweet friend" she replied. "Now, would you like to reach the enchanted water?" she asked with a smile.

I felt very humbled and didn't really know what to say. I did want to see around, in fact I couldn't wait to see what was in there, but at the same time I didn't want to intrude in a special place.

"Dawn, my sweetest friend, I admire your thoughtfulness not wanting to intrude but this is for anyone who needs it and I would love to show you around" she said.

Argh, I keep forgetting about them being able to hear my thoughts. I ought to be careful what I think about I laughed to myself.

"Frangel Briadh, thank you for having me, I'd love to come in, please can you open the gate for me" I asked her.

"It doesn't open" she laughed.

"Do I need to call Jeremiah to fly me over?" I enquired as I looked around to see where he was.

"No, no, no, you can do it all by yourself" she said.

Gee this place wasn't half confusing I thought to myself. But I trusted everyone in it. Well apart from the Wartons, but I didn't even know who they were!

"Dawn, only those who truly want to do good will get past the gate. I need you to concentrate on your breathing for me and see yourself, in your mind's eye, being on the other side of the gate." She instructed me "If you are truly a good person who wants to help others and not hurt them you will get through the gate."

I suddenly felt nervous but stood still, breathing my relaxing breath, with my eyes closed. I kept visualising myself on the other side of the gate and as I let my third breath out I heard a voice telling me to open my eyes - I was on the other side of the gate. This place was better than any story had ever told and better than any movie could make. It was beautiful and I felt like I belonged here and that was before I even ventured right into the place. Now I understood why Frangel Briadh was excited to show me this place. It was full of life. I stood for a few minutes just taking everything in, filling all my senses with my surroundings. I could hear the birds singing to each other and I was pretty sure I could understand what they were saying. No, I must be going mad. I am not a bird, I don't speak bird language I thought to myself.

"You don't need to Dawn and yes you *can* hear us, you are not imagining it" tweeted one of the little robins in the tree.

"Is this the only place where you can hear the animals? I've never heard them anywhere else in the World Of Light."

The little robin told me to look around and tell him what I noticed. All I could feel was love and peacefulness and looking around all I saw was a very beautiful and magical place.

"Look closer" tweeted the robin.

As soon as he said it I realised I was in the middle of a rainbow and everything around me was indigo in colour. Each new thing I saw in this magical World Of Light left me breathless with wonder and thinking that it couldn't possibly get any more magical, yet I was continually being shown more amazing things. I felt so lucky to be part of this incredible world. It was so far from the earthly world I knew.

"Can you guess what this magical area is called?" Jeremiah asked me.

I had no idea but could guess it was something to do with shells. There were shells everywhere. The huge area of water was shaped like a giant shell. It had a small waterfall at the top end and all around the outside of the water were hundreds of tiny little shells. I could've spent days just looking at the shells themselves. Each one was a different shape, size and colour. They all shimmered like they had glitter on them. The water was like a mirror – it was so still and reflected each shell. The small waterfall at the top had a little pond of its own to catch the falling water. As I got closer I could see that the water was more than just a mirror – it was so clear that I could see every shell and pebble on the bottom of the water.

Jeremiah told me it was called the enchanted water and he persuaded me to go to the water's edge.

"I..... I......I don't know what to do" I told him.

"You just need to stand directly over the water, anywhere, and look in it, the magic of the water will do the rest for you, but you must really want this change before you look into it."

I did want to, so I stood over the water and gazed into it. The water went from being see-through to being a mirror again where I could see my reflection. As soon as I saw my reflection I was drawn into it like a magnet. Even if I wanted to look away I don't think I'd have been able to. I saw my reflection in a huge ripple of water, like a circle of light around me. As I continued looking at myself in the water the ripple started spinning around, slowly at first then gradually getting faster. The circle of light spun with the water, rising as the whole circle rippled and spun like a tornado. My reflection was replaced with bright white light and I felt like I was in a spinning whirlwind of pure white light. My heart felt so full of love that I thought I was going to pop like a balloon and I felt so much peace inside me. It was like a piece of chocolate that was dissolving as all negative bad feelings and stresses just melted away from me and instead I was being filled with this incredible love and light.

"This is what beautiful is, it's not how you look, but how you feel inside. When you have only love in your heart to share with everyone you meet *that* is beautiful. When you meet someone, even just for a few minutes, and leave them feeling better than they felt before you met them, *that* is beautiful. Beautiful is the way we are born and it's sad that people's experiences in life can take away that beauty. This enchanted water is the magical doorway that gives back the beauty that we all have inside of us, but we can't always reach. Anybody who chooses to find their beauty within can come here to this special place, but they have to want to change before the magic of the gate will let them through. You can't trick your way through, it won't work" Jeremiah whispered to me.

I felt love pouring from every pore in my body. I knew that deep inside I was a good person and I never wanted to hurt anybody, but I guess it's easy to lose who you really are when you are in the middle of so much anger, hatred and fighting. I felt like I was really me again, but an even better version of me than I'd ever been.

I wish I could help everyone feel this way and help them find the beautiful person that is deep inside.

"The fact that you want to help everyone shows just how beautiful you are Dawn, but you will never change everyone in the world, no matter how much you want to or how hard you try. But if everyone in the world helped just one person to see the light inside them we would all make the world a better place together" Jeremiah told me.

"Then I want to change one person. No, not change, I don't want to change anyone, I just want one person to see the beauty inside of them and for them to want to change themselves. I want to help just one person see it, feel it, feel what it really feels like to feel beautiful. Truly, deeply beautiful." I said really meaning it.

Maybe I could help one of these Wartons find their beauty I thought to myself.

CHAPTER SEVEN

I lay in my bed thinking about the night before and couldn't stop smiling. Mirabriel helped me believe that I really could do something with my life, and that it wouldn't always be this horrible. She even showed me that what we were living through may help us somehow in the future. Almost as if there was something hidden from us, like the gold in the wall, but I couldn't see it or reach it. It made me excited knowing life could get better. It gave me hope. I lay smiling, lost in the World Of Light and flying with my Frangel sister, trying to work out how I could help just one Warton change from being horrible to beautiful, when Mum came storming into my room shouting that I was going to make myself and Danny late for school. I got such a fright that I burst into tears - something I rarely did. Mum looked shocked and stopped yelling for a minute.

"What are you crying for?" she asked.

"I don't know Mum. I don't want to get Danny or me into trouble but I didn't know what the time was and you gave me a fright" I sobbed.

Mum put her arm around me and sat next to me on my bed. "Dawn, I shouldn't have shouted, I'm sorry. It's not your fault, but you know what will happen if your Dad gets up and you're both still here," she said in a hushed panicky voice.

"I wish he didn't have to be so mean," I snapped and stormed out of my room to the bathroom. I grabbed a towel and cried into it so Dad wouldn't hear me crying. I cried until I ran out of tears, washed my face and went back to my room to get dressed. Downstairs, I found Danny grabbing the last banana for breakfast. No breakfast for me then. Again! Mum tried to hug me and Danny stopped in his tracks as he saw me push her arm off, telling her to leave me alone.

"Dawn, there's no need..." Mum started, but I cut her off before she could finish.

"It's always my fault Mum. It's my fault if we are late, it's my fault if Danny's not ready, it's my fault if Dad hears us talking, it's my fault for everything. Well, Mum I've had enough, it's not my fault that he's so mean, it's not my fault he hits you all the time, it's not my fault I hear you screaming and begging him to stop - even when you don't think I can hear you, I can and I do. It's not my fault you don't believe that you can take us and run away from that bad meany. None of it is my fault so why don't ...."

But before I could finish I saw Dad out of the corner of my eye. He was only wearing his boxers so he must have heard me screaming at Mum and got out of bed. Before I could say or do anything I felt his hand on the side of my face. It hurt badly, but I was so shocked I couldn't say anything. I just ran out of the house and kept on running. I heard Mum shout my name but I didn't look back. I had no idea where I was going, I just kept on running.

I knew what I'd been saying before he appeared and I knew he'd be angry. What if he was running after me, what if he was going to do it again? He'd be mad that I ran away. Mum was probably getting my punishment right now. Oh no, what about Danny, I'd left him in the kitchen too. I should go back. Mum wouldn't be able to protect him. She's never protected either of us so there is no way she'd be able to protect Danny now. But if I went back I'd probably make it worse. I didn't know what to do so I just kept running. I could hardly breathe, I was so frightened. I knew what Dad was capable of and that's what scared me. But I was also scared that Danny or Mum would get it. I couldn't see the ground, as my tears made it look all hazy. I started to feel dizzy looking at the blurry ground which was moving fast beneath my feet. Suddenly everything went black.

I had no idea how long I'd been lying there but when I woke up my head was bleeding and I was surrounded by trees, with Danny standing over me crying and begging me to wake up. I was confused. Why was I lying down? Why was Danny crying and where was I?

"C'mon Dawn, get up before Dad follows us," Danny begged.

I suddenly remembered what had happened, though I still didn't know where I was.

"Where is he? Where are we? How did you find me?" I asked as he pulled me with his tiny hands until I managed to get onto my feet.

"I left him at the house and followed you. I kept shouting but you didn't hear me. Come on, if we run we can get to school on time. We need to hurry though in case he followed me!"

I got up and found my balance and realised that we were near the bus stop. I must have been going to get on the bus and taken a short cut past the trees, though I don't remember it. Danny told me there was a huge tree root at the side of my head. I must have hit my head off it when I fell over, knocking myself out. We could hear the school bus coming.

"Run!" Danny shouted, but I was still dazed and confused. He dragged me by the arm but it was too late, the bus had just driven past. Danny started crying again, panicking that Dad was going to come after us.

We decided to take a short cut that Dad was unlikely to know about. It still meant we'd be late but it was better than going back home. Dad would go mad on both of us, it wasn't worth it, it would be better to get into trouble at school for being late.

As we hurried through the woods Danny told me that after I ran out of the house he waited a few minutes before running after me as he heard Mum tell Dad that he shouldn't have hit me. But Dad just got really angry and told Mum that I'd better look out when I got home. Danny was scared and said that we couldn't go back.

I told Danny we needed to tell someone what was going on at home but he wasn't happy.

"There's no point. You know Mum told us never to tell, and if we did it would be so much worse for us," he said.

"Yes, but those people told us before that they could help keep us safe, and you know if we go back home we are not safe."

"No, no, no. No way!" Danny shrieked. "You heard Mum. She told us that's what they'd say. We can't trust them, you know that. Mum has told us so many times. We'd just be taken away from home and I'd never see you again."

"Well, yeah, and that would be a good thing," I snapped. "Well, apart from not seeing you. But we won't get split up, they'll keep us together. I only got a slap this morning. You've seen what he does to Mum so can you imagine what is waiting for us?"

"Okay fine, Dawn, you go ahead and tell someone. But don't come crying to me when we get told Mum's dead as Dad has killed her and we were not there to stop him," Danny snapped. We walked the rest of the way to school in silence.

We got to school about twenty minutes later and went to the school office. The receptionist Mrs Kelly was really nice and didn't give us a row after we told her we'd missed the bus and had to walk. She took us to our classes where my teacher, Mrs Thomson, was nice too.

Everyone was looking at me when I walked in, whispering and giggling. I wished they knew how sad they made me feel when they did that. I'd already had a horrible morning but I still went into class smiling and cheerful like nothing was wrong. If only they knew just how close to the edge they pushed me every time I heard a giggle as they looked at me or heard them whispering my name as they talked about me.

Today was no different from any other day. Apart from my two friends, Peggy and Lola, everyone else laughed at me, so I was used to it. It made me feel sad inside most days, but today it made me want to run and run and keep running and never come back. I didn't let them see that they bothered me. There was no point, they wouldn't care even if they did know. It was okay for people who went home to families who loved them and wanted them. Just because I never told anyone what my life was like at home didn't mean I wasn't hurting really bad inside. As I went to sit at my table I heard someone behind me giggling. I tried hard not to cry, but I couldn't help it. The lump in my throat came up and my eyes watered but I somehow managed to hold the tears back. Nobody was going to see me cry in school and have another reason to make fun of me. I put my head down and started reading the book everyone else was reading. As the bell went for play time Mrs Thomson asked me to stay behind.

Everyone walked past me, laughing, a few of them prodded me in the side or nudged me as they walked past. Just because I didn't react they thought they could keep on pushing and pushing until they broke me. What they didn't know was that I was already broken, they just couldn't see it. I'd had no sleep because of the fighting all night, nothing to eat, my face and head hurt and as usual I'd probably have no tea or if I did it would be very little. Then the night's fighting would start all over again. School was the only safe place I had, but it wasn't really that nice a place anymore. My friends Peggy and Lola said I was being bullied, but I never saw it like that. I just saw it as people, who didn't understand what was happening to me, being horrible. I really hoped that none of them ever have to live the way that Danny and I were living.

Mrs Thomson asked me if everything was ok. She was such a lovely person that I almost believed that she really cared, but she was nice to everyone and I knew that she was paid to be nice so just because she was nice to me didn't mean anything. I wasn't going to fall for that.

"Yes, Mrs Thomson. I'm so sorry I was late, we missed our bus," I muttered without looking at her.

"No, no, my dear, it's quite alright that you were late. I was just worried about you. What happened to your face?" she asked in a concerned voice.

I was scared and didn't know what to say. I must have looked nervous as she touched the back of my hair and told me I had blood on it.

"Errrmm. I fell," I said very quietly.

She sat next to me and told me again that she was worried about me.

"It's okay, I did fall Mrs Thomson, my Mum and Dad would never hurt me. I hit my head off a tree root when I fell and that's why we were late," I said, relieved that I had a real story and didn't have to make anything up.

She told me that I'd better get it looked at by the school nurse. I would rather not have, but on the other hand I was actually quite glad as my Dad would go mad if he saw my hair covered in blood.

Mrs Thomson took me to the nurse's room and told me to sit down whilst she fetched the nurse. At first the nurse seemed like a scary lady. She was so big that I was frightened just looking at her. But she was funny and made me laugh, she made me feel relaxed. She was round and had short grey hair. It looked like it was blonde in bits but mostly grey. She wore a navy blue dress and looked very grumpy. But once she spoke she had the softest, sweetest voice. She was about the same age as my granny – not that we were ever allowed to see my granny.

I realised that just because someone looked scary didn't mean that they were. I mean, just look at my Dad. He looks like a friendly kinda guy. When he speaks to people outside of our home he comes across as the nicest person, so it just shows how wrong you can be when you judge someone by how they look. I'd heard so many kids laugh at how the nurse looks and say how much they don't like her, but that shows they don't even know her. If they bothered to get to know her they would see how nice she really was.

"There you go, sweetie pie," she said, "That's you all cleaned up." She put her hand on my arm and smiled as she looked at me. "You can come and talk to me anytime, sweetie pie." She let me go with a smile that made me feel cared for.

By the time I left her room it was nearly time to go back to the classroom. As I was walking past the head teacher's office I heard my name being spoken and Mrs Thomson say "I'm really worried about her, that mark on her face does not look like an accident and she looked very worried when I asked her about it."

I wanted to keep listening but I kept walking in case they caught me. I felt sick and scared. Please, oh please don't tell my Mum or Dad I begged inside my head.

I dreaded going back to class, but nothing was said. Lunchtime came and went and I started to get nervous at the thought of going home. I tried to let my school work distract me, but it didn't work too well. I kept thinking about how Dad was going to react when I got home.

I wasn't able to focus on what the teacher was saying so I just looked down at my desk so she thought

I was reading the book, hoping she wouldn't ask me any questions. I remained lost in my thoughts when I became aware of all the sounds of the classroom disappearing and I heard someone talk to me.

"Hey I'm Frangel Yosmig and I want to take you to the Frangels meeting place" came the voice of a Frangel and I suddenly found myself in the World Of Light. We were in the middle of lots of green hills with nothing other than nature around us.

"Woah, how did I get here?" I asked not waiting for an answer. This place was better than school any day.

"As you can imagine the meeting place is very special and not just anyone can go, in fact it's a place that not many people know about. It has to be guarded from the Wartons or they could do much harm" Frangel Yosmig continued.

I was so excited that I ran around in a circle, punching the air. I was going to be taken to the Frangel meeting place. Me? Really? Wow! "Yes, yes, yes, I feel amazing and life feels so good when I'm here. I am so lucky, thank you" I finished as I somersaulted onto the ground.

Frangel Yosmig giggled and suddenly lots of little Frangels appeared around us.

Frangel Mirabriel appeared in front of me. "These extra special Frangels only show themselves to those with beautiful energy, I hope you can see just how beautiful you are" she finished.

I was flabbergasted. The place was alive with Frangel magic with hundreds of little lights all around the Frangels as they walked.

"You sure you want to go to the Frangel meeting place?" she checked with me.

All I could do was nod with a huge smile.

"Ready......? Let's go" Frangel Yosmig said excitedly as we all took flight and hundreds of wings lit up the air with their bright white lights. As the hills in the distance got closer, we started to lower. At first all I could see was the green of the grass, but the lower we got the clearer and bigger the small castle became. It was surrounded by lots of stones, all different shapes, around the castle.

"We're not stopping here, we just wanted to show you Castle Ewen. This is the rocky tower where we watch over the glen to protect it.

"Who is Glen?" I asked assuming it was a man I didn't know.

Mirabriel appeared and chuckled "Glen is not a person, a glen is the Scottish name for a valley and Castle Ewen is a rocky tower which gives us the best view of the glen where the Frangels are working" she informed me.

The rocky tower was surrounded by purple heather, which was very beautiful with lots of little hills which looked like cones. I drank in the colours and the energy, it felt so good. We continued to fly over the glen until we reached Trotternish ridge, which was a big hill with lots of tall jaggy rocks, splitting the hill into different sections. From above I could see lots of Frangels working, all doing their different jobs. The hill lit up as everyone busied themselves with their individual tasks. They all seemed to have their own white light around them, maybe they were wearing head torches I thought to myself.

"That is what you call an Aura my sweet child" Frangel Sorina introduced herself as I landed on my feet.

"It's....it's...it's so lovely to meet you. Thank you for having me here" I stuttered in amazement, taking in the beauty of the place.

Frangel Sorina informed me her job was to ensure the Frangels remained protected as they worked and because she could read people's aura she was the best Frangel to help keep them safe from the Wartons.

"You are a very special child indeed my sweet one. Not many people can read auras" she smiled at me.

"I don't understand. I don't even know what an aura is" I informed her confused.

She smiled as she put her arm around my shoulders. "My precious child we all have our own unique energy which forms an egg shape around us. To most people it's invisible, but some very special people can see it. It is made up of different layers and a good energy – a nice person – has a nice white light around them, amongst other colours. But someone who wishes badly upon others can have black around them. So, when you read an aura it means you can see the colour around that person and have an idea as to what kind of energy they have around them at that time."

"Is that why I see the Frangels with lots of little white lights around them, is that their aura I see?" I asked.

"Indeed it is my dear" Frangel Sorina confirmed.

"So, how can I learn to read them?" I asked, hungry for more.

Frangel Sorina gave a warm smile as she told me that seeing the aura comes naturally to me, I don't need to learn it but in time I would discover what each colour meant.

"But how can't I see that in the earthly world?" I asked "Is it only Frangels who have aura's?"

"No, no my dear, everyone has an aura. But sometimes in the earthly world there are too many worries and stresses that it can be hard to focus on feeling and seeing other energies. Because you have spent time here in the World Of Light you have been able to *just be* without thinking or worrying and that is what has allowed you to develop the natural abilities you have." She explained.

Not sure that I really understood I thanked her anyway. What did she mean by *just be*, surely if I was alive then I *was* just being I thought to myself? Maybe she meant I was a human being I tried to reason.

With that thought a funny looking Frangel appeared, introducing herself as "Frangel Habetrot."

"I can teach you what *just being* means" she offered.

She was dressed in the strangest of things. She had lots of stuff hanging from her, bells from her waistband, spools of thread from her hat, measuring tape around her like a belt and many other strange items. She giggled as she heard my confused thoughts and told me to follow her. We flew up and over some of the small encircled areas of the hill and landed in a section enclosed by jagged stones. There was a real fire burning in the corner, lighting up the place which was decorated with lots of hanging jumpers and scarves everywhere, all of different sizes and colours. In the middle was a rocking chair which sat on a rug of purple heather, making it very cosy. It was dark by the time we got there and the sky was so clear I could see the blanket of stars above us.

Frangel Habetrot stood very still whilst looking into the burning fire. I didn't speak because she looked as if she was somewhere else as she gazed into the flames and I didn't want to disturb her. After a few minutes she turned to her right and looked up to the stars with the same gaze that she was looking intently into the fire with. Looking up, her hands were doing something mid-air, which was mesmerising to watch. She began pulling something out of the sky as she continued gazing upwards. I had no idea what she was doing until I saw lots of silver appear in her hands. She continued to pull a stream of silver out of the sky and as I looked up I could see a line of silver stars coming out of the sky and into her hands as she slowly moved them in all directions, moulding the silver into the shape of a chair. Then suddenly she snapped out of her gaze and put the seat she had just made onto the purple rug of heather next to her rocking chair and she ushered me to sit down.

We both sat on the chairs in front of the fire. My chair looked as if it was made of glistening silver stars yet it felt like I was sitting on soft cushions.

To the left of the rocking chair was a large machine which Frangel Habetrot described as a spindle for her wool which she used to knit her jumpers. She told me that her jumpers had magic knitted into them and anybody who wore one would feel better and heal from any ailments.

"Now Dawn, I am going to teach you how *to be*. All you need to do is watch the flames of the fire as you listen to your heartbeat."

"But I can't hear my heart beat" I informed her, not wanting to seem ungrateful for her help.

"For now, I want you to *just be* and that is what I'm going to teach you." She handed me a green jumper and I could see now that all the other jumpers that she had hanging around the place were different colours of the rainbow. I put the jumper on, sat on my chair and started to watch the flames, just as Frangel Habetrot had asked me to.

"If your mind wanders, just listen to your heartbeat and focus on watching the flame." I couldn't hear my heartbeat but I did as she told me. After just a few seconds of looking at the flames I could hear a loud beating in my chest. I put my hand to my heart and watched the flames. I felt quite emotional, as if my heart had been let out of a cage. I had got used to not letting myself feel anything as it was less painful that way. I kept focusing, listening and watching. I could see the flames dancing in the slight breeze. I had no thoughts in my head at all. I was just watching and listening. I heard Frangel Habetrot tell me that was what was meant by "*just being*" – being in the very moment and not thinking about or doing anything. It certainly was a very peaceful place to be. I liked *just being*.

I was lost in the flames of the fire as the blanket of stars wrapped themselves around me. I've no idea how long I'd been there, but I was jolted back to reality when I heard my name.

"Dawn, did you hear what I said?" Mrs Thomson gently asked me.

"N… no, I'm sorry," I admitted as I looked down in panic, noticing that I still had the green jumper on which Frangel Habetrot had given me.

"Mr Mackintosh wants to see you in his office."

All at once the whole class said, "Ooooooh, Dawn's in trouble" in teasing voices.

"Quiet!" Mrs Thomson snapped.

I wasn't totally surprised, I was half expecting it. But why did she have to say it in front of the whole class? The head had probably called my Mum and Dad by now. I felt sick as I walked to the office. I thought about running away - it had to be better than what was coming to me when I got home. Where would I go? How long would it be before I got found and put back home? That would just make it so much worse. No, I decided I had to just take whatever came to me. I guess if I got it then Mum would probably get a break from it, so maybe it would be a good thing, even if it did hurt. I knew Dad would be all nice to the head teacher – Mr Mackintosh would never see through him. Dad was far too sneaky to let you see him the way he really was. He was good at fooling people.

On my way to the office I looked down, remembering the green jumper that Frangel Habetrot had given me was still on. I raced to the toilet where I quickly took my school jumper off and put it back on again, trying to hide the green jumper before making my way to the head masters office. On the way I saw Danny in the corridor going to the toilet too. He was wearing the same jumper that I had just been given, but in blue. I panicked "Danny get your jumper off, quickly, before we get into trouble for not being in uniform" I whispered. "Anyway why were you in the World Of Light when you should be in class?" I demanded as I pulled at it with my fingers. He looked at me and pointed as he told me that he couldn't take it off and if I could go to the World Of Light then so could he.

"Anyway, you can't talk, look at you. You are wearing your jumper so why should I take mine off?" Danny retorted.

"I left it on under my uniform so you can't see it" I told him, "now go get it off."

"Dawn, look in the mirror dumb dumb, it's not under your clothes, it's on top. Look, its green I can see it." He snapped at me.

I looked down, he was right, even though I'd put my school jumper on top, my green jumper was still there.

Danny's favourite teacher was approaching us in the corridor. We both looked at each other in panic "Let's just get out of here before she notices anything" I said as I grabbed Danny's arm and walked in the direction of the class he should have been in.

"Is everything ok?" she asked.

"My......my jumper.... but before he could finish the Eagle Warrior of Light appeared on top of Danny's head and wrapped his wing over Danny's mouth to stop him from talking.

"Yes everything is ok, thank you" I informed her "I was just helping Danny clean his jumper as he had spilled something on it" I finished as I tried to cover his tracks, grabbing him by the arm "I'm just making sure he gets back to class Miss" I finished as I pulled him away.

"What was that for?" Danny asked when we got out of her earshot.

The night warrior told Danny that nobody could see our jumpers apart from the two of us.

"Aaaahhh that was close then" he chuckled.

"Danny how many times do I have to tell you, don't tell anybody anything about the World Of Light"

I scolded him "You are going to spoil it for us and it's not funny."

"I know, I know, but I get so excited sometimes that I get carried away and forget" Danny defended himself.

"Why is your jumper blue, anyway?" I asked him, forgetting about what Frangel Habetrot told me.

"One of the Frangels gave it to me and told me that we all have something special inside of our bodies that help keep the energy in the body in good health and balanced or something like that and the colours all have special jobs to do. Blue is to help me speak the truth about how I feel so I can stand up for myself more." Danny said beaming.

"That's awesome, I get it, but now get to class, hurry up" I ordered him.

CHAPTER EIGHT

I reached the head's office and knocked on the door.

"Just a minute," Mr Mackintosh shouted.

I stood there for what felt like hours. I tried to hear who was in the office but all I could hear were muffled voices. The longer I stood there the sicker I felt and the closer I got to actually running away. Eventually I told myself I'd be safer to run away. How much worse could it be than living the way I did? I finally knew - after he hit me - that Dad really didn't care, and that Mum couldn't or wouldn't protect me, so I'd be better off somewhere else. I was sure I'd find food – it's not that I got much to eat at home anyway. I'd probably find more than just a banana in the street. I could steal from a shop. No, I couldn't do that, it's wrong. But I could go in and ask nicely for something. Maybe someone would feel sorry for me and let me have something to eat. Sleeping wouldn't be a problem as I never got much sleep anyway. All the shouting and fighting kept me awake half the night, so I was sure that I could easily find somewhere to hide and sleep for a couple of hours.

Just as I was about to turn around and run away Mr Mackintosh opened his door, "Dawn, come in," he said, smiling. I felt sick and my legs were wobbly.

There was a lady wearing bright coloured clothes with dyed red hair on one chair and a lady with black trousers, white top and black jacket with her hair in a ponytail on the other. Where were Mum and Dad? There was no-one else in the room.

"Dawn, these two ladies would like to talk to you," Mr Mackintosh said. "I'm happy to stay with you while you talk, or I can get another teacher to sit with you if you want?"

I shook my head "I'm ok, thank you" I managed to say, just wanting it over and done with.

"Ok, but I'll only be in the next room. You just need to ask if you want me, or anybody else here with you, and one of these ladies will come and get me" and with that he left the room.

They both smiled and told me to sit down. It was as if there was nothing to worry about and I wasn't in trouble, so I sat down. I remembered this happening before. Mum had asked me a thousand questions after I had got home, making sure I hadn't said anything and reminding me never to tell anybody anything about our home life.

"Dawn, my name's Emma, I'm a social worker and my job is to speak with children" the one with the bright hair said. She was smiling and I noticed she had a hoop through her nose, like the ones you see in bull's noses.

"My name's Mary and I'm a police officer, but you're not in any kind of trouble, none at all," she said "like Emma, one of my jobs is to speak with children as sometimes they have things they want to tell me."

I've heard this before, I thought. I just nodded, looking at the floor. For what felt like ages they tried to tell me that I was in a safe place to talk and that it was okay to tell them about anything that may have been worrying me.

When I heard Mary say the word "safe" I looked up from the floor for the first time. Something made me believe her. But I was still scared. I remembered Mum telling me that's what they would say, but all they really wanted to do was tear our family apart.

It was the same thing they'd told me before, but that time I had got into so much trouble from Mum when I got home because she thought I'd told them something. And that was when I'd said nothing, so I couldn't even begin to imagine the trouble I'd get into if I actually said something. But I guessed it couldn't get any worse, so I thought maybe I should just tell them everything and get me and Danny out of there.

The Mary lady told me that the video camera which was sitting on the desk was recording everything that we were all saying and doing. She told me that they were going to record the interview because everything I said was important to them and they didn't want to miss anything that I may have to tell them. She told me that I didn't have to speak with them if I didn't want to and that if I didn't want them to record it then they would switch it off.

I felt so scared and confused. Should I believe Mum and say nothing or believe them and tell them everything? But if they record it then they may show it to Dad and he will know I have told them everything. Oh Mirabriel, I wish I knew what to do. I started to cry.

All of a sudden I was blinded by a light and felt warmth on my shoulder. "My dear sweet child, I love you and will always be here to help you. Fear not, you are not alone."

My tears stopped suddenly and I could hear the lady with the bull nose and the other lady talking to each other wondering what I was looking at. I realised that although Mirabriel was in the room, sitting on my shoulder, they couldn't see her.

I heard one of them ask me to tell them about myself, but I was too concerned with what I didn't want to tell them to focus on what they asked.

"I don't know what to do Mirabriel, Mum tells me one thing, and they tell me something else. They make me feel safe, but Mum always told me it was all pretend so they could break up our family."

"Dear child, speak to me in your thoughts, unless you want others to hear you. They can't hear or see me, but they can hear and see you. Visualise your jumper turning blue, that will give you strength to speak" She said then disappeared as I realised I'd just spoken out aloud.

"Dawn, what did your Mum tell you?" the bull nosed lady asked.

I put my hand over my mouth and shook my head. How could I have been so stupid? I couldn't believe I had spoken out aloud. I was such a fool, I kicked myself. Well, I'd just lie and hope they believed me. Oh I hated telling lies – I was never any good at it.

"My Mum never told me anything," I said.

"Who were you speaking to Dawn?" the other lady asked.

"Nobody," I lied.

"Who is Mirabriel?" the bull nose lady asked.

I jumped up, panicking. How did she know Mirabriel's name? Had she seen her or heard her? I'd thought she was our friend, she'd told me that only Danny and I could see her.

"I don't know what you are talking about," I said.

"You spoke to 'Mirabriel' and told her that you didn't know what to do, Dawn," the bull nose lady said. She seemed kind and spoke so gently.

"Did you see her?" I asked in a panic.

The ladies shook their heads. Phew! I was happy, I really could trust Mirabriel. I imagined my green jumper turning blue, as Mirabriel had told me to.

"Who is she?" the Mary lady asked.

"Who's who?" I asked. I wanted to confuse her so she'd forget.

They looked at each other. "Mirabriel, who's Mirabriel?" the bull nose lady asked.

"I don't know."

They looked at each other again, then back to me. Thankfully they decided to let it drop and didn't ask again. The bull nose lady came closer to me and put her hand on my arm as she crouched down next to me. She looked into my eyes and told me that she cared and wanted to help me and that it was okay to talk if I wanted to.

I was so confused. My heart was crying inside but nobody could see it. I wouldn't let anyone see it. I was worried that if I let anyone see or if I let my sadness show that it would never stop. So I just kept it all in.

"Dawn, tell me about yourself?" The Mary lady asked me.

"What do you want to know?" I asked not knowing what she wanted me to tell her.

"Tell me what it is like to be Dawn."

"Well …..I live at home with my brother" I said not knowing what else to say.

There was a long pause before Mary lady spoke "Tell me about your life at home with Danny."

"How do you know my brother's name?" I demanded.

"Dawn, we are here to listen to you both," she reassured me, without answering my question.

I stopped thinking of myself and thought about Danny's frightened face and the thought of Dad hitting him. I couldn't bear the thought of Dad hurting Danny too. I felt the anger well up inside and without any further thought I blurted it out "I hate my Dad and I hate living at home!"

I saw the look on the two ladies faces and realised what I'd done.

"Tell us about it, Dawn," the Mary lady said.

I knew I shouldn't have said anything and I clammed up. What had I been thinking of? I am so dumb I berated myself.

"There's nothing to tell," I told them. I was in for it now. Dad was going to make me pay for this, I knew it.

They asked me to tell them what life was like at home, I couldn't tell. It would just make it so much worse for all of us.

"Dawn, I know you're scared, but we are here to listen to you. Tell me what happened to make you hate your Dad" the bull nose lady said.

I stopped thinking because I believed her and for some reason I trusted her and with that I decided to protect Danny and Mum too.

"My Dad slapped me," I blurted, then started to cry. I cried so hard I couldn't breathe or see, but I was aware of people moving around the room. I had no idea what was going on but I felt the gentle touch of the bull nose lady's arm around me. I put my head into her chest and she hugged me. I couldn't remember the last time I'd had a hug from anybody. It felt so warm, and safe. For a moment, I forgot where I was, I just lay in her warm embrace feeling safe.

She asked me if I was okay and if I wanted to carry on. I did, so I told her what had happened that morning and how I'd been late for school because I'd fallen. She kept telling me that I was doing well and asking me if I was okay to keep talking. She asked me about life at home, so I told her. I told her everything. She told me she was so proud of me for being able to tell them.

"What about my Mum and Danny?" I sobbed, unable to stop crying.

"Don't worry, Dawn, we are going to do all we can to make sure that you, your Mum and Danny are safe" she reassured me.

I started to feel scared at what would happen next, but also excited that I wasn't going to have to live like that anymore.

"Will you make sure my Dad's taken away forever so he can't ever hurt any of us again?"

"You've been so brave telling us everything, Dawn, and I'm going to do everything I can to make sure your Dad can't hurt you ever again." Her voice was reassuring.

CHAPTER NINE

I didn't go back to class afterwards, I stayed in the nurse's room for what felt like forever. I wished they would just come and tell me that Dad was gone. I had lots of thoughts running through my head and a tiny part of me was scared that Mum was right and they wouldn't believe me.

I heard the school bell go for home-time and I was still sitting in the nurse's room with no idea of what was going to happen. I decided to go to Mr Mackintosh's office to see if he'd forgotten about me. I got to his office door, which was slightly open, but not enough to see inside. I knocked on the door.

"Just a minute."

I didn't say anything, I just stood there. I could hear the bull nose lady and the Mary lady speaking, but I couldn't really hear what they were saying. They sounded upset. What was going on? I looked at the clock and it was nearly 5 o'clock. I should've been out of there and home hours ago. I was scared as I didn't know what was happening. The only thing I knew was that they were going to get Dad out so I guess I didn't want to complain too much.

A few minutes later Mr Mackintosh opened the door slightly and I heard him say, "You'd better do something."

He looked surprised when he saw me standing there. "Dawn, how long have you been standing there?" he demanded.

"Only a few m...m... minutes," I stuttered, suddenly nervous about his reaction.

"Did you hear us talking?" he asked.

"N....n...no, honest Mr Mackintosh, I promise I wasn't listening in, I was just wanting to ask if those ladies got my Dad out of the house yet so I could go home."

"Oh, okay Dawn. I'm sorry, I know you've been waiting a long time, hopefully we won't be much longer. I'm speaking to Emma and Mary just now. If you have a seat back in the nurse's room one of them will be down to get you shortly."

I went back to the room, as I was told to. They never told me it would take this long. As I sat down Mirabriel appeared in her bright flash of rainbow stars. She jumped onto my knee and stuck out her tongue, making me laugh.

"That's better my sweet child, much better to see you laughing," she smiled.

"What's going on Mirabriel?" I asked.

"My beautiful child, I am so proud of you. You have done such a brave thing today. You are so strong looking after your Mum and brother, I know today hasn't been easy for you" she said as she jumped onto my shoulder.

"I don't feel very good right now, I feel scared," I said, tears starting to roll down my cheeks again.

Mirabriel jumped on top of my head and peeked down my forehead as she looked into my eyes giggling.

"Come on, let's go to the WOL!" she said.

"Go where?" I asked confused.

"The World Of Light – if you take the first letter of each word it spells WOL so I sometimes call it the WOL" Mirabriel giggled "Now, come on let's go play" she said.

"B....b... but what if they come back?"

"Trust me," she said. The next thing I knew I was standing next to Frangel Briadh, who was making candy floss.

"Dawn!" she screamed and ran towards me to give me a hug that lifted me off my feet. We giggled together.

"Here, have some candy floss," she said, handing me a giant multi-coloured candy stick. "Put your stick in there and twirl it around," she giggled.

I did as she told me and before I knew it my candyfloss was the size of a balloon. Frangel Briadh took some sort of scooshy sauce and poured it onto my candy floss. She was giggling so much that she made me giggle too.

"Go on, try it!" she said, still giggling.

I did as she asked and as I ate it my feet started lifting off the ground.

"Wooaahhhh!" I panicked, but the panic didn't last long. Within seconds I was giggling again and feeling so light and free from any worries or fears. In fact, I forgot I even had a Dad I was so happy. My life at home was forgotten about, as it always was when I got to the WOL.

Frangel Briadh was standing below me, laughing. She clicked her fingers and all of a sudden I fell to the ground.

"Ouch!" I said as I landed with candy floss stuck to my face.

Frangel Briadh was laughing so hard that hundreds of little gnomes came running out from inside the trees to see what was so funny.

The whole place was filled with the sound of laughter, so much so that all I could do was laugh too. Frangel Plum ran in front of me with a camera and took a selfie of the two of us. She showed it to me, and I looked so silly I could see why they all laughed so hard.

"Why is everyone so nice here, why doesn't anybody argue or hit each other?" I asked Frangel Briadh.

"Dawn, I'll answer your question but let's travel in magical style" she said as she snapped her fingers and Jeremiah and Dreamer appeared. We mounted our unicorns and glided through the WOL.

We rode over lots of different parts of the WOL, I'd had no idea it was so big. I didn't understand why I had to go on a unicorn for my question to be answered, but I didn't mind. I was just so happy, I wanted to live here forever and ever and ever.

We arrived at a big cave-like place where there were hundreds and thousands of ants. They were all running about very fast, talking to each other.

Dreamer and Jeremiah gently lowered themselves to the ground and stood still. I watched as the ants worked together quickly, they looked like they were building a castle.

"Yes, they are," Frangel Briadh said as she heard my thoughts. "Watch how so many of them all work together. They all know what needs to be done. They build their own homes before the winter, each one has a special job to do and they work together to get the work done."

I was amazed watching them work together.

"Now watch these two here," Frangel Briadh said, pointing to an ant with a striped baseball cap and another wearing a yellow belt. I watched as they squabbled. "Get off and get back to your own space," the one with the cap yelled to the one with the belt. I giggled as they got annoyed with each other.

Frangel Briadh kept looking at me. "Do you see? There are squabbles here, but that's normal in life. What is not normal, Dawn, is for people to hit each other, or shout at them in anger or call each other horrible names," she said. "Dawn, what happens in your house is not normal, it doesn't happen in every house and, most importantly, it is wrong. It's so wrong what your Dad does to you all." Frangel Briadh spoke in the most serious tone I'd heard her use.

I looked down to the ground, stroking Jeremiah "So why does it happen in my house?" I asked.

"My sweet child, Dawn, lots of things happen in the world that are wrong but they are not your fault. It doesn't mean you're not a good person, because you are a good person, you are a very beautiful person, with a good heart. What your Dad does is so very wrong and it should be stopped. Your Dad knows he can get help with his anger, but he chooses not to. Until he decides to get help, you should not have to live the way you do. What you did today by telling those ladies was an incredibly brave thing to do.

Telling on an adult is the only way you can get help to make it stop. Your Dad needs to get help from someone for his anger. He needs to learn how to deal with it and not take it out on you, Danny or your Mum or anybody else. The only way that can happen is if your Dad decides to get help or you tell an adult just like you did today." She smiled at me.

Jeremiah reared his head and made a loud 'neigh' as if he was agreeing with us and we both giggled.

"Thank you," was all I could say. "I love it here, I love not being scared and I'm not scared here at all."

Frangel Briadh smiled. "Come on," she said "we've only just begun this journey." She started counting.

"One, two, three, let's ride above the trees." She clicked her fingers. We lifted off the ground and for the first time I noticed Dreamer and Jeremiah had wings.

"Wow, I love it here, I love you, Frangel Briadh, and I love Jeremiah and Dreamer and I love Mirabriel for taking me here!" I said aloud.

Frangel Briadh just giggled again. She threw something at me shouting, "Catch!" It was a ball and we started playing catch in mid-air while the unicorns rode with us above the trees. I was laughing and giggling so hard as the unicorns flew faster, making it more difficult to catch the ball. When the ball dropped Frangel Briadh just clicked her fingers and another ball appeared. I don't ever remember laughing so much!

"Now let me show you something else" she said as we flew through the clouds. "Dawn we are going to go into the yellow of the rainbow and I need you to change your jumper to yellow. As we go through the yellow stripe I need you to concentrate on breathing in the colour yellow" she instructed me. "We are all going to be invisible, so I can show you what life is like in the Warton pod" she informed me.

"B...b... but last time Jeremiah went invisible we were in the red stripe of the rainbow" I said confused.

"Indeed you were, but the difference with yellow is it will make us invisible to the Wartons but we can still see each other" she clarified.

I did as she told me and we flew over an area covered in lots of large rocks. We stopped above the Warton pod and hovered mid-air as Frangel Briadh told me to just watch. She told me she wanted me to see what they were capable of just to get into the light pod. I watched three of them running around then suddenly turning to stone, just like I'd seen before. Now I could see what they were planning. If they turned to stone nobody would know that it was a Warton and they could sneak their way into the Light pod. I also saw some of them change into different animals as part of their trick. One of them even turned into a tree. These Wartons really were very clever yet so very horrible and sneaky. Why can't they see that being kind felt so much better than how it felt to be nasty I thought to myself.

"Frangel Briadh can I try to speak to them, to tell them how much better it feels to be kind. How it feels to truly feel beautiful inside?" I asked her.

Frangel Briadh shook her head and said it wasn't a good idea as all the Wartons would hear what I said.

"Please, just one of them?" I pleaded with her.

"This could be dangerous Dawn, but I will let you into a special secret" she replied. "If you change your jumper to all the stripes of the rainbow you can become invisible but one person who you choose to focus on will be able to hear you and you will be able to hear them, but nobody else will hear the conversation apart from that one person you intend it for."

"Oh thank you, thank you Frangel Briadh" I said gratefully. I wanted to try and help just one Warton to see and feel the beauty inside of them. I sat in silence for a few minutes, just watching them. One Warton in particular caught my eye as he seemed to run about the most and seemed the most determined to cause as much damage to the WOL as he possibly could. I even watched him change into a butterfly so he could try and trick me into thinking he was Mirabriel. He was surrounded by a black cloud, which must be his aura. I don't think I'd ever have fallen for his tricks because I'm sure his black aura would have alerted me. But I felt sorry for him because he was determined to cause so much unhappiness that he must feel very bad inside himself. So I decided to try and focus on him. I called him Rockflower because he must have had a heart of rock to be so unkind but I wanted him to be as beautiful as a flower so I thought Rockflower suited him perfectly.

"Hey Mr Rockflower" I called from the air above him as I sat on Jeremiah.

Nobody seemed to notice or hear me except Rockflower himself who was looking around to see who had just spoken to him.

He actually heard me, I chuckled to myself.

"Hey Mr Rockflower, yes you Mr Warton who just changed from a rock to a butterfly and back to yourself" I said as I let out a giggle. I knew I shouldn't have but I couldn't help it.

He jumped up and looked all around him but never saw anyone near him. I could see he was worried but trying to appear cool so he didn't look stupid in front of his Warton buddies.

"Why are you so unkind?" I asked him seriously.

He jumped up shaking "Wh....who.....who's there? Who is that?" he asked looking everywhere but seeing nothing.

A few of the other Wartons ran over to him asking him if he was ok. They all looked around and told him he was imagining it as there was nobody there.

I changed my jumper back to yellow so I was still invisible but I could speak to Frangel Briadh. I laughed and laughed so hard that Frangel Briadh couldn't help but laugh too. We laughed until we nearly stopped breathing.

"Now, I hope that will stop him trying to hurt other people" I said as I changed my jumper back to rainbow stripes ready to speak to him again.

It didn't matter where I was, as long as my jumper was rainbow striped and I focused on the person I wanted to speak to then it would work, Frangel Briadh told me.

"Please try to be kinder to other people" I said as I watched the little Rockflower jump again at the sound of my voice.

"No need to be afraid" I told him "unless you keep living the miserable life you are choosing to lead now" I finished.

"Who is this?" he asked.

"All you need to know is that I can see you, which means I can also see the bad you do. You don't have to be mean, nasty or miserable you know. You have the choice to change and I can help you" I told him.

I watched him run and hide behind a huge rock with his hands covering his ears.

"I told you I can see you and speak to you even if you run and hide, that won't make any difference" I told him.

"What do you want? Who are you? Go away" he shouted.

I wasn't finding this funny anymore because I really wanted him to change. I thought if I could persuade him to change then he could change one other Warton who could then change one other Warton and so it would go on until there were less unkind people left.

"If you really want to change then all you need to do is tell me and I will show you how to change" I told him.

He was shaking with fear as he stayed hiding behind the rock.

"I'm going now, but I'll be back to see if you have thought about what I have said. Remember I will see all the bad you do. Choose wisely" I said as I closed my eyes and changed back to the yellow jumper.

"I'm ready to go now Frangel Briadh" I said "Thank you for allowing me to try and help him" I said as we left the Warton pod.

"I am very proud of you Dawn. You are a very beautiful person you know. Now I have somewhere else I want to take you" she said as Jeremiah and I followed Dreamer who was flying at speed, landing on the ground a short time later.

CHAPTER TEN

I was lost for words. This place was incredible. I saw lots of little bright coloured mini caves scattered through the forest, with animals running about everywhere. There were birds flying and deer running about playing with each other. I watched two snails sit opposite one another with a rainbow between them, coming out of each of their antennae. I'd never seen a rainbow made by snails before. Two birds flew to the rainbow which the snails had made, took an end each and flew away with it. The snails immediately made another rainbow. They obviously didn't mind the robins taking it as they seemed quite happy to carry on and make another one. I wondered where they were taking the rainbow to as they disappeared out of sight and when they did come back a short time later, they never had the rainbow with them, instead they went back to the snails looking for more. Another rainbow disappeared with the birds and another rainbow was made.

"Jeremiah, what are the birds doing with all of these rainbows?" I asked, hoping that he was somewhere close enough to hear me.

Within seconds he appeared. We all have the ability to help here in the World Of Light, *"watch,"* he said, as he bowed his head, pointed the horn on his head forward and lots of rainbow stars came from his horn forming a perfect rainbow. Within a few seconds two birds flew past us, chirping as they picked up an end of the rainbow each and flew away with it. I was speechless. Did I just imagine that? Or did it really happen I thought to myself?

"No, you didn't imagine it" Jeremiah told me. "Watch, I'll show you again" and once more Jeremiah produced a magical rainbow from his horn and another two birds immediately appeared and flew away with it.

Jeremiah laughed at my bewildered, yet amazed, look. This is where all the rainbows are made to send down the rainbow chute to earth to help those who need it. Can you imagine how many people are healed with all those healing colours beaming down onto them? Jeremiah commented.

"I once needed blue to give me strength and as soon as I changed my jumper to that colour I had lots of strength" I confirmed.

Well it's the healing colours of the rainbow that are helping people on earth feel better so we all do our bit in the WOL to help make each rainbow in our own magical way" he finished.

As I looked around I saw two fish pop their heads out of the water and form a rainbow between them before they went back under the water again after the birds took it away. All over the water there were rainbows being made by the fish. I'd never imagined so many rainbows flying over a water surface, it was majestic.

There were squirrels in trees making rainbows between each other, elephants with their trunks reaching out touching each other forming rainbows. Everyone seemed to take some responsibility in helping and I felt so very happy watching them all.

I'd love to know how they get the rainbow to earth to help people, I thought to myself. Seconds later I felt a surge of energy as I saw myself surrounded by white light lifting me off the ground.

"C'mon, help us then" came the unfamiliar voice. I had no idea who it was but I could hear lots of different kinds of bird song.

As we flew up high I could see the area was surrounded by rocks and rainbows everywhere. The whole place was lit up and glowing, it was so beautiful and full of life.

A robin flew right by me and told me that they would take me to the rainbow chute which sent the rainbows to those who needed them. We were high enough for me to see the whole of Trotternish and I could see all the different Frangels doing the jobs they were asked to do. It was such a busy place. I saw the rocky tower in the distance and Frangels and animals were scattered all over the blanket of purple heather as they were travelling back and forth to Trotternish.

There were little white lights everywhere. Suddenly I noticed three Frangels walking with a deer by their side. It wasn't like any of the other deer who were running about the place, this one was different. Instead of being surrounded by white light this was surrounded by black. It made me feel very uneasy and I just had a bad feeling about it. I called to the robins and told them what I saw and they both immediately let out a bird call. It wasn't their normal tweets and seconds after they called out hundreds of birds and other animals surrounded the deer whilst the Frangels who were with the deer ran away.

I don't know what happened but as the birds and animals surrounded the deer it disappeared. I've no idea what they did or even why they did it but I knew it couldn't have been a good deer.

I suddenly realised I was floating in the sky on my own as the robins who were carrying me flew away and the rainbow which they were carrying slowly descended over me. Everything looked violet and I could hear what all the animals were saying

"That girl has a real gift" one said.

"If it wasn't for her that Warton may have got into the rainbow pod and shut it down" said another.

"That was close, everything could've been destroyed" said one of the rabbits.

"Those Wartons are so sneaky" croaked one of the frogs.

"I agree, I've seen them change into many things and many different animals but I've never seen them turn into a deer before" said another deer.

"They would never have got past Aunt Morgana though" said a wise little robin.

Lots of animals agreed with the robin but they all repeated how well I did to stop him when I saw him. If that was a Warton then it was lucky that I spotted it but I had no idea that is what it was, I just thought it was a deer, with a black aura, though I knew there was something not right with it. I just didn't know what it was. I wondered where it went.

As I was lost in my thoughts the two robins returned and picked up the rainbow again. The world was striped for a second as they lifted the rainbow back over my head. It went from being violet to indigo, then blue, green, yellow, orange, red then the world looked normal again. *Wow this is my stripey world and it's pretty awesome* I thought to myself. I'd stopped hearing what the animals were saying and we continued flying, with them singing again. Frangels were busy below us, some even flying past us, lots of birds flying everywhere, with and without rainbows. Looking up ahead, I saw a huge hill which we were flying towards.

As we got closer to the big hill the birds began flying faster and singing louder as they changed their song to a different tune. We flew around the top of the hill in a circle three times, as they tweeted their new tune and as we'd finished the third circuit, the top of the hill swivelled to the side, exposing a huge hole in the ground which was dazzlingly bright. I've no idea how many rainbows were inside there, but they were everywhere. The two robins tweeted even louder as we hovered above and the world was striped once again as we lowered ourselves into this amazing place. I was going through rainbow after rainbow and chuckled as I heard all the different animal conversations.

Inside the hill was a huge oak tree. There were rainbows on each branch which glistened like twinkling lights on a Christmas tree. Mirabriel appeared next to me, giggling as she told me she would race me to the bottom of the tree. I watched her race ahead of me as she used each rainbow as a chute and slid down from branch to branch until she reached the bottom of the tree. She did beat me, but I sure had fun bumping and sliding down each rainbow. I looked up from the bottom of the tree and it looked enormous. There was a door at the bottom of the tree trunk.

Naturally I was curious to see if it opened, so I pushed the door and to my surprise it opened to reveal a room filled with rainbows. Magical is the only word I could think of.

"Go on then" Mirabriel urged me.

I followed the spiral staircase, which was made out of a giant rainbow, down inside the tree trunk. Any other time I would have found this scary, but I didn't, quite the opposite in fact. The spiral stairs seemed to go on forever and I experienced every colour of the rainbow as I went with it. At the bottom two robins came flying past me with yet another rainbow.

"Ah, just in time, so you are" came the voice from the bottom of the stairs.

I looked around trying to find the voice but all I could see were sparks of light.

"I've been looking forward to meeting you Dawn" came the same voice.

Sparks everywhere, white, green, blue, actually they were all rainbow colours. They sparkled everywhere, flickering faster and brighter until eventually all the sparks formed the outline of a person.

"Who, what are you? Do I know you?" I asked.

This time I knew the voice came from the sparks but I didn't know who or what it was. Was it a person, or an animal? I had no idea.

"My name is Aunt Morgana and I make sure we send rainbows to the right people who need them in the earthly world" she said.

"I can't see you properly" I replied.

"My sweet one, you can see so much more than most people. To most people that I am around I am invisible and they can't even see the lights that you are seeing. You have a very special gift and an open mind that allows you to see me" she finished.

I was speechless. Me? Special? Well I never saw myself as that, that's for sure.

"You....you.... you look like you are made up of diamonds, lots of twinkling sparks of light. Is ....is.....is that what you look like when you look at yourself?" I asked curious to see if I was seeing properly.

Aunt Morgana laughed as she told me she was made of light.

"Would you like to see how the rainbow pod works?" she asked me.

"I feel very special and incredibly lucky that you would want to show me. Yes, I would love to see it, please" I replied gratefully.

"Watch over there" Aunt Morgana said as she pointed her finger to the tree where a huge circle magically appeared, hanging from the lowest branch. It looked like a spider had spun a web inside the circle and it had crystals in the middle of it, with beads and feathers hanging from the bottom of the circle. The web slowly disappeared as the middle of the circle sparkled with bright light, which got brighter and brighter.

"Watch this dream catcher screen and you will see what I can see in the earthly world" she informed me.

Aunt Morgana must have seen the confused look on my face as she explained that what I was about to see is what Mirabriel did for me.

"So, really, what I am about to show you is what I see inside my head" she clarified for me.

I was bewildered but I had no time to think about it as a little boy appeared in the middle of the circle as if he was on a TV screen. He was hiding down the side of his bed crying.

"Ok, next rainbow ready for delivery please" Aunt Morgana called.

Two robins appeared with a rainbow and hovered next to a door in the floor, which Aunt Morgana pointed to, causing it to burst into sparkles of light before opening. One of the robins went flying down through the door with the rainbow. The other robin flew back up the tree and the rainbow door closed.

The boy on the screen was still crying when Aunt Morgana said "Ok, watch.......right........now" and with that a rainbow of stars appeared on top of the boy, showering him with bright rainbow light. The boy jumped up but quickly sat down again, staring in amazement. His tears stopped and out of the stars appeared a Frangel who introduced himself to the little boy and told him not to be afraid as he was there to help him. And with that Aunt Morgana, who had been sitting with her eyes closed, opened them and the dream catcher disappeared.

"We don't need to invade their privacy any longer, what they say to each other is private and between them now."

"So my sweet Dawn, this is how the rainbow pod works" Aunt Morgana informed me.

"What will happen to the robin? Will he come back?" I asked curiously

"The robin will now become that little boys' Frangel"

I was completely overwhelmed. I didn't know what to say until I found myself saying

"Thank you for sending me a rainbow and a robin."

Aunt Morgana came over to me, twinkling in light and put her arm around me. I couldn't see it but I felt her there, I felt such a peace that it was as if I was floating until I looked down at the floor and realised that I was floating.

"Oops!" Aunt Morgana giggled "I forgot about the effect that I have when I touch people. My energy can be quite overpowering and I really ought to remember that" she finished with a chuckle.

She moved her arm away from me and I felt my feet touch the ground again.

Suddenly I was back sitting in the nurse's room and I heard footsteps coming towards the room I was in.

CHAPTER ELEVEN

I felt a little confused, only a minute ago I was in the World Of Light and now I was back in school. But I knew where I'd been and what had happened over there so I had to forget about it for now, pull myself together and act normal. All my worries and fears came flooding back to me. I sat in the chair as the bull nose lady and the Mary lady came in, both looking very serious.

"Dawn, we can't take you home just yet, so we have a lovely lady who is going to take you out for your dinner," Mary said. At that point a lady walked into the room. She looked very sweet, like somebody's Granny and she smelled like she had granny perfume on too. She was tall and slim with white hair tied up in a bun and she wore a black and white checked skirt, a black blouse and a red and green scarf. "This is Margaret," the bull nose lady told me.

"Why can't I go home?" I asked.

"We just have a few things we need to sort out first, Dawn, so Margaret will take you to get dinner. You've done so well today, you should be very proud of yourself," the bull nose lady said.

"I just want to go home. Where are my Mum and Danny?" I asked feeling frightened.

"Please don't worry, Mary and I are going to be speaking to your Mum and Dad whilst you're having your dinner," bull nose lady said.

She gave me my jacket and Margaret came over and put her arm around my shoulder.

"C'mon Dawn, tell me where you'd like to eat. Your choice, wherever you like." Margaret smiled and squeezed me close to her. I didn't know her but I felt safe, but also very afraid of what was going to happen.

Margaret took me to my favourite place to eat – McDonald's. She even let me have a milkshake as well as chips and a burger. Last time I was at McDonald's was when I was four years old. I remember it really well and ever since I've kept asking to go back, but the answer's always been the same, "We can't afford it." Dad could always afford his drink, though. He never had to go without, that's for sure.

Margaret seemed like a lovely lady. She spoke to me for a long time as we ate. I wanted to hug her she was so nice. The bull nose lady and the Mary lady had been nice too, but there was something different about Margaret, something very special.

She said she understood how scared I must feel and that I could talk to her about anything. I told her what Mum told me about not saying anything to anyone, and Margaret said that's because Mum was frightened about what Dad would do and that Danny and I would be taken from her.

She explained that when adults do something they know is wrong they will sometimes tell that person something bad will happen to them if they tell anyone. Margaret said it didn't happen with all adults, but it happened with lots of adults who did bad things that they knew they shouldn't do. She told me that what Dad did to Mum, Danny and me was wrong and that no adult should ever make anybody scared of them or hit them. She said my Dad needed help. I told her that I thought that was just what happened to everyone. Surely being hit was normal? She said I felt that way because I didn't know any other way to live. It was all I'd ever known, so I wasn't to know that there was any other way. She said if I lived in her house for a week I'd soon see that what happened in my house was not normal. She said in her house they all cared for each other and tried to make sure that they all felt safe and happy, not scared and sad. They may fall out and disagree with each other, but nobody ever got hurt, not deliberately.

"Can I come and live with you?" I asked.

"Oh Dawn, I'd love nothing more than to give you a happy home so you could feel safe, but I'm afraid it's not that simple." Margaret said, looking sad.

"Please?" I begged her.

I knew she would make me safe. I felt safe just sitting beside her and talking to her. I knew she was telling the truth. She didn't say any more about it, but I knew by the look in her eyes that there was no changing her mind. How I'd love to have her as my Mum, I knew she would protect me.

We finished our dinner and she asked me if I'd like a Mcflurry. I didn't know what that was. I thought it was her way of telling me we had to go in a 'hurry.' When she explained that it was an ice cream we both chuckled. I couldn't believe what she came back with. It was the most amazing ice cream ever. It had little bits of chocolate inside it. I don't remember the last time I had chocolate, I think it was the chocolate bar I got for my birthday two years ago as I don't remember having any since then.

Margaret watched me as I ate. She didn't want one. Wow, how could anybody not want one of these I thought? I ate it so fast my head started to hurt.

"Brain freeze?" Margaret asked.

"My brain has frozen?" I panicked.

"No, no, that's what you call the pain in your head when you eat something cold very quickly" she chuckled.

Margaret told me it had been her birthday the previous day and she'd gone out for dinner with her family to an Italian restaurant.

"How did you get to Italy and back in one day?" I asked, amazed.

"No, we didn't go to Italy, we went to a restaurant that cooks Italian food" Margaret chuckled.

"Was it nice? What did you have?" I asked, being nosey.

"Well, I had a lovely Italian pizza then an ice cream and I had brain freeze too when I ate mine!"

We laughed. It was fun to laugh, to really laugh - great big belly laughs. They made me feel happy inside. Margaret made me feel happy, even though I didn't really know her, I felt safe being with her.

"What did you get for your birthday?" I asked being nosey again.

Margaret showed me the beautiful watch she was wearing, "I was given this and I also got perfume, a new jacket and some chocolates."

"Wow!"

I couldn't believe someone could get so much for a birthday. For my last birthday I'd got a cup with my name on it. That was such a beautiful gift for me, I loved it. I heard the other kids at school talk about getting lots and lots of parcels to open on birthdays and Christmas. Most kids seem to get more each Christmas than I had for all my birthdays and Christmases put together.

Last Christmas I got a pretty red dress. Danny got a nice blue shirt. We never got any other parcels from anywhere. But that was the way Christmas always was, we got one parcel each. I used to wonder why the movies always showed lots of parcels under a tree. I thought they were really rich to get more than one present.

Margaret's mobile rang and she walked away from our table to answer it. I heard her say, "Okay, I'll take her there now." She came back to our table and explained that I had to go to see a doctor. She said it was nothing to worry about, but because I had a mark on my face the doctor wanted to check I was okay.

As we walked back to Margaret's car she explained that it wasn't the hospital I was going to, but it was a house which the doctor used to examine little boys and girls. Margaret must have seen the fear in my face as she immediately tried to reassure me that there was nothing to worry about.

When she stopped the car I asked if we were at her house, but she told me this was where the doctor was going to examine me. It was a house in the middle of lots of other houses and definitely not where I would have expected to find a doctor. Margaret told me that nobody lived there, they just used it to speak to people and for the Dr to examine people.

We got out of the car and Margaret put her arm around my shoulder and smiled at me. She told me I was doing well and that she was proud of me. Those were words that I'd only ever heard from Mirabriel and the bull nose lady.

We went through the front door and met the bull nose lady and the Mary lady. They told me I was doing really well and that the Doctor had already arrived. They told me that whilst they were speaking with her I could look around the house.

It was just like a normal house. There was a living room, a kitchen, a bathroom and a playroom full of toys. There was a magic mirror in the playroom, which looked like a mirror when you were in the playroom but when you went into a small cupboard in the hallway the mirror was actually a window which looked into the playroom.

The last room she showed me was what she called the doctors room. It was empty so I knew Mary lady and the bull nose lady must have finished talking. The room had one of those beds that you get in the Doctors surgery which had curtains around it so no one could see you. There was a big machine at the bottom of the bed, but I didn't ask what it was for.

I finished looking around and went back into the living room, where everyone was waiting for me. There was a lady I didn't recognise. Margaret put her arm on my shoulder and told me that it was the doctor who was going to examine me.

"Why am I getting examined?" I asked "What does it mean?" I looked at Margaret feeling very scared. So many new people everywhere and I should have been home hours ago.

Margaret squeezed my shoulder as the doctor lady came closer and shook my hand.

"My name's Rachel, Dawn, and I'm a doctor. There's nothing to worry about, all I'm going to do is have a look at that mark on your face and I'll look at the rest of your skin. I'll check your weight and height and that's about it. That's all an examination means – just looking at you to make sure there's nothing to worry about and to check you're healthy. But I'll only do it if you agree. Nobody's going to force you to do anything you don't want to do. Okay?"

"Why are you all being so nice to me? Why do you care?" I asked, feeling confused that strangers would care about me.

I saw the bull nose lady look at the Mary lady.

Margaret pulled me close to her and said, "We're nice because we care, we care because you are a lovely little girl who deserves to be cared for, like every boy and girl."

I tried to hold back the tears, but I couldn't any longer. Nobody had ever showed me they cared before, not the way all these people had today. I ran to the playroom and sat in the playhouse.

Margaret came through with Doctor Rachel and asked if I was okay. Doctor Rachel told me again that I didn't have to do the examination if I didn't want to.

I was sobbing. "I'm just not used to anybody caring about me, that's all. It feels weird, but kind of nice."

Doctor Rachel told me that every child should be cared for and looked after but it doesn't always happen. Sometimes it takes other adults to realise that a child's not being cared for to do something about it.

"What are you going to do to help me?" I asked as I dried my tears, feeling a little better. Maybe life could be happy. If I lived with any of these ladies I'd be happy, I knew that for sure. I love my Mum but I was starting to think that she didn't really care, if she did she'd have got us out and away from Dad. But she hasn't, so she can't care, I thought to myself even though deep down I knew she did.

Doctor Rachel asked me if she could examine me in the doctor's room, she told me that I didn't have to do it if I didn't want to. I agreed to go through with her. She asked me if I wanted someone in with me. I immediately looked at Margaret and went over to put my hand in hers and we walked through to the doctor's room.

Doctor Rachel filled out lots of forms then looked at my legs and arms. I had to take my top off but she gave me a blanket to keep me covered and warm. Next she looked at my legs and weighed me on the scales and measured how tall I was. She asked me how I'd got the mark on my face and I told her about my Dad hitting me. She took a tape measure and measured how big the mark was and wrote it down. Once she had finished everything she told me how well I'd done and said I could go into the playroom for a while. I heard the bull nose lady and Mary lady go in and speak to her. They were in there for ages.

When they came out I asked them when my Mum and Danny would be home so I could go back home too. They looked at each other and said they had a few phone calls to make and Doctor Rachel left. Mary lady took photographs of the mark on my face. She held a silver "L" shaped ruler next to it which she said was to show how big the mark was.

I didn't understand why I couldn't just go home. I'd done all they wanted me to do. It seemed like ages before they came back. Margaret stayed with me in the playroom and we drew pictures.

The Mary lady came to the door of the playroom and asked Margaret to go out of the room with her. I heard them both talking outside the door and I carried on drawing my picture for Mum.

Margaret raised her voice. "What do you mean no evidence?" I knew something was wrong because she sounded upset. I didn't know what 'evidence' was so I had no idea what they were talking about.

The Mary lady and bull nose lady came back into the room and Margaret came over and sat beside me. They didn't look as happy as before and I knew something wasn't right.

"What's wrong, what have I done?" I asked.

The bull nose lady told me that they were ready to take me home. I was so happy I could have cried. We can be happy at last, I just knew it. I couldn't wait to see Mum and Danny.

"Dawn, your Dad will still be there," Mary lady said.

"What do you mean? I can't go until he's left! You told me, you said you would help me. I trusted you to make sure I was safe. You don't understand, he'll be mad and safe is the last thing I will be. So mad that I can't go home until he's gone! I just can't! I trusted you to help me" I said again, panicking in total fear.

CHAPTER TWELVE

Mary sat down and explained that Danny and my Mum wouldn't tell them what had happened that morning. They both denied seeing anything. She said they spoke to Dad and he'd said that he hadn't hit me which meant they couldn't take me away from the house.

I didn't understand.

"But my Dad did hit me. You saw that mark on my face, I told you what happened. Why don't you believe me? He is lying, why do you believe him?" I asked.

I looked at Margaret and saw she had tears in her eyes. She looked like she was about to cry, but she didn't. She put her arm around me and explained that with everyone else saying it didn't happen they didn't have enough evidence to take Dad away.

"Evidence!" I shouted "I don't even know what that is, but I do know my Dad is going to be so mad and if you put me back home he will beat me up good and proper just like he does to Mum all the time!"

They all looked as if they felt sorry for me but I didn't care, they weren't going to get what I was going to get when I got home. They'd tried to make me feel better by saying Mum and Dad would have to go to lots of meetings with social work to prove I wasn't being treated badly, but that didn't mean anything. What about all those other times they weren't at the meetings, what then? Who was going to protect me then 'cos Mum sure wasn't going to? She can't even protect herself from that monster.

"You must know that we do believe everything you have told us, Dawn. I promise you, we do. This isn't because we don't believe you," the bull nose lady said.

"If you believed me you wouldn't make me go back to him. Not unless you just didn't care. You're just like everyone else. If you really believed me why would you put me back to a house where you know I am going to get beaten up? So you either don't care or you don't believe me! I trusted you! I trusted you both!" I screamed in the direction of the bull nose lady and Mary lady.

I pushed Margaret's arm off my shoulder and ran out of the room. I locked myself in the bathroom and cried until I had no more tears. I heard Margaret speaking to me through the door, but it didn't mean a thing. I should have kept my mouth shut and not told anybody anything, Mum was right all along - I wouldn't be believed. But I didn't listen to her and now I was going to have to deal with Dad. I looked to my left and saw an open window. *Perfect* I thought. I don't need to go home at all.

I pushed the window right open and jumped out. I had no idea where I was going, but I knew it wasn't home. I ran to the bottom of the garden and found a path. I ran and ran and kept running until I had no breath left and could run no more. Mirabriel appeared in front of me, telling me that I needed to go back to the house. She said everyone was worried about me.

"Go away," I told her as I kept on running "Nobody cares." My legs hurt and I could hardly breathe but at least I wasn't near Dad. I'll never go back there. Never!

I don't remember much about where I went or what paths I took but I knew I'd gone through lots of gardens, over a few roads and through a park. I came to a pond with ducks in it and I stopped as I couldn't run anymore. I sat down next to the water to get my breath back. It was dark but I was too out of breath, angry and scared to worry about where I was.

A few ducks waddled up to me as I sat there. If they were looking for food they could forget it 'cos I didn't have any. But they just sat next to me, almost as if they knew I needed a little friendly company.

I sat for what felt like hours and felt a little better when I got my breath back and my legs had stopped hurting. But it was dark and I was starting to get scared. All I could see were lots of trees and the edge of a big field. There was nobody around apart from me, the ducks and darkness. I lay down next to the two ducks, I was so tired.

I don't know how long I'd fallen asleep for, but I woke up freezing cold and surrounded by darkness, so dark that I couldn't even see the trees anymore. There were no street lights and no houses. Just darkness.

"Oh Mirabriel, I'm so scared," I said out loud. But I'd told her to go away so I didn't expect her to come back when I called her. I guess I didn't have any right to even ask for her after being so horrible.

The duck pond lit up with a bright white light and Mirabriel appeared in a dazzle of rainbow stars. "My dear sweet child, I have never left you, I am always by your side, even when you can't see or hear me. I will always look after you and make sure you are safe." She was so bright it looked like there was a torch shining out of the middle of the water.

I started to cry. "Oh Mirabriel, I'm so scared. I don't know where I am, where I'm going or what I'm going to do! I just had to escape. I couldn't let them put me back there," I sobbed.

"I've been watching them, they are all very worried about you, Dawn. Let me guide you home," Mirabriel said.

"No, no way! I'm not going back, not now, not ever! Dad will kill me!"

"Anyway Dad won't be worried, he won't care. Mum and Danny won't care, they lied to the police and social work. That Mary lady and the bull nose lady won't care, they were going to put me back home even after I told them everything. The only one who really cared was Margaret. I heard her get angry when they told her that I was going back home, but she's already told me I couldn't live with her, so what's the point. Nobody cares!"

I stood up and started to walk away.

I'd only stomped about ten paces when I stopped because it was too dark and I couldn't see where I was going.

"Oh, Mirabriel, I'm so scared" I cried again.

"Come back and sit down and let me speak with you," Mirabriel said as she stuck out her tongue, making the whole place light up with falling rainbow stars that tumbled out of her mouth. She made me smile, I loved it when she did that. I did as she asked and sat back down. I was still too angry and upset to listen, so Mirabriel told me she was going to teach me how she calmed herself down when she felt angry or upset. I didn't really care, if I was being honest, as she wasn't feeling what I was feeling but she had been so kind to me and she was all I had right now so it felt only right that I listened to her.

"Okay, this is what I do – I think about nothing else other than my breathing and count in my head. Watch me.......... as I breathe in I slowly count to five, then I hold my breath and slowly count to five again, then I let it out slowly as I count to five" Mirabriel told me as I watched her breathing slow right down.

I nodded to show her that I understood what she was doing and I was delighted that it worked for her but I had no idea why she was telling me that right now. I certainly couldn't see how that would make me calm. Mirabriel asked me to sit with my legs crossed, my hands on my knees and breathe at the same time as her.

"Breathe in… one… two... three... four... five…

"Now hold it… two… three… four… five…

"…and let it out… two… three… four… five…"

I did as she asked and thought we were finished but she did it again and again. Then she asked me to count in my head as I was breathing.

I breathed in, counted to five, held my breath for five and let it out for five. I don't know how many times I did it but it definitely worked. I felt much calmer and all my anger had faded.

"Now, my sweet child, you know how to calm down. You can do it anytime, anyplace and nobody

126

even needs to know you are doing it, but it will help calm you."

I was very calm but I got bored counting and started to panic again. "Mirabriel, what am I going to do? I'm too scared to go home, especially now I've run away, it'll be even worse. Why did nobody believe me? Why does nobody want to help me?" I asked.

"I know this is going to be hard to understand, Dawn, but they do want to help you," Mirabriel said.

"But they told me they'd make sure I was safe. Taking me back home to Dad isn't making sure I'm safe" I whispered. It was so quiet that I could hear frogs croaking and the ducks gliding in the water.

"Mary, Emma and Margaret did all they could to help you, Dawn, as did the doctor. But they have rules they have to go by and that's what they did," Mirabriel said.

"What rules?" I snapped.

"Dawn, your Mum and Danny are so afraid of your Dad that they said he is a good man…"

Before she could finish I interrupted, "Why would they say that? They both saw what he did to me, they know that is not true."

"Do you remember the first time a social worker spoke to you, Dawn? You told them a lie, you told them everything was fine at home. Do you remember?"

I put my head down and nodded, "I was too scared of Dad" I said.

"Exactly, sweet child, and that is why your Mum and Danny said the same thing tonight, they were both too afraid."

"The police spoke to your Dad and he denied everything. He also tells lies, but he tells them because he doesn't want to get into trouble," Mirabriel tried to explain.

"So, because nobody has told the truth, apart from you, that breaks the rules the police and social workers have to go by. It's not that they don't believe you but because there are three people saying it didn't happen and one saying it did, they have got to have a really good reason to take you away from your home. The red mark on your face had faded by the time the doctor saw it, otherwise it would have backed up what you told them. Those rules are what they call 'evidence.' They needed more evidence to be able to keep you away from your Dad." Mirabriel explained it in a way I kind of understood.

"So I should have just said nothing then and it would have saved me from getting into so much trouble."

"No, you did absolutely right Dawn. Even though they can't take you away, your Mum and Dad will be watched very closely by social work, and if anything like this happens again you will be taken away," Mirabriel said.

"No I won't, they'll just lie again!"

"Dawn, I am fairly sure that today Danny was too afraid to speak out, just as you were the first time you spoke to the police and social work. However, after he realises that by telling the truth he *can* be helped I am sure that he won't make that mistake again." Mirabriel explained "he will have learned from you that you can go to a teacher, you will be believed and they *can* do something to help you."

It made sense, I guess. "So, what now?" I asked. "I'm in even more trouble now for running away, what do I do?"

Just then another very bright light appeared with the giggles of Frangel Briadh.

"Hey, Dawn, it's only me" she giggled as she watched me jump in fright.

My heart was racing but at the same time I was elated that she was here.

"I've just popped by to tell you that everyone is so worried about you that you won't be in any trouble, I betcha!" she said.

"Where did you come from? How long have you been there?" I asked.

"Dawn, Dawn, Dawn. Hey, I'm your Frangel sister, I'm just like Mirabriel, I'm always by your side keeping you safe even when you can't see or hear me," she said.

That was pretty cool, I was happy with that. I heard lots of noises coming from the bushes. I was about to start running again, I didn't care where I ended up. I wasn't going home and I wasn't waiting to see what the noise was either. It could be Mum or even worse it could be Dad. I jumped up and started to run. I had no idea where I was going, nor could I see because it was so dark. I heard a man's voice. I felt like I was going to be sick, I was so scared. If that was Dad, then I'd never be taken home alive. He'd beat me like he beats Mum. I just knew it.

I didn't know where Mirabriel or Frangel Briadh went and I didn't stop to look, I just kept on running.

"Ouch!"

I tripped on something and hurt my leg. It was really sore but the fear of Dad got me up on my feet and running again. I could see the reflection of the moon on the water so I knew I wasn't going to fall in.

The man's voice got louder and louder. He was catching up with me and it was then that I realised that there was more than one person chasing me as I heard the pounding of feet. I was breathing so hard and fast that I nearly couldn't breathe at all. The beating of footsteps got closer and closer so I threw myself into some bushes, hoping whoever it was would run past me.

CHAPTER THIRTEEN

All of a sudden there was a vicious dog in front of me, barking so much that I was sure I was about to become his dinner. I immediately stood up and stayed very still but he was still barking and jumping up on his back legs as if he was going to take a chunk out of my face, but despite his fierce bark he never bit me or even tried to. A bright torch shone on me and I heard a man shouting "BUDDY COME" as he shouted at me that it was okay, he was a policeman. I didn't know if I should believe him or not, why would his dog be so mad at me if it was true? Mirabriel appeared mid-air in front of me and told me that he was telling the truth. The police dog had to bark to let the policeman know that he'd found me. She told me that it was ok to trust this man then she disappeared.

The man caught up with his dog and I heard voices on what I thought must be his police radio. He shone his torch and I could see he was in a police uniform. I was initially relieved because I thought he would keep me safe, but I'd also trusted the Mary lady and she was putting me back home where I wasn't safe, so maybe his appearance meant nothing either.

I started to run again but it was pointless as the dog immediately ran after me, barking, making me freeze again.

The policeman shouted "Good boy Buddy" as he threw a ball for his dog to fetch. I was glad he'd stopped barking and I stopped crying. The man told me his name was Craig, he was a policeman and his dog was called Buddy and together they had come to find me as everyone was worried about me. I was so sure nobody would find me and I was annoyed that he had.

"How did you know where I was?" I asked curiously.

Craig smiled and said that was what his dog was for, to track my scent.

"You mean he smelled me? Do I smell?" I asked.

Craig chuckled. "No, you don't smell bad, but everyone has their own scent and even though we can't smell it, a dog's nose can. What's your name?" he asked.

"Dawn."

The radio on his jacket lit up and I heard him say he'd found the misper.

"What's a misper?"

"It's short for a missing person"

"Am I a missing person?"

"Nobody knew where you were, Dawn, so yes you were missing" Craig said.

"Yeah, like anybody cares," I muttered quietly. But obviously not quietly enough as Craig quickly scolded me and told me that my Mum and Dad were very worried.

I laughed out loud when he said that.

"Worried? Yeah right, worried I'd get Dad into trouble more like. I could be dead for all they care. Now please go away and leave me alone." I cried and started to walk in the dark.

Craig followed me with Buddy, who was no longer barking.

"Dawn, I understand that you must feel afraid, upset, angry and frustrated but sometimes things happen that we don't understand, however there is almost always a reason for them. We don't always see it at the time but in time we come to see just what that reason was." Craig said this in such a caring way that I nearly believed him.

"You sound just like Mirabriel" I said.

"Who?" Craig asked.

"Oh never mind, it doesn't matter." I'd spoken out without meaning to. "What would you do if your Dad beat you up and you watched him beat up your Mum every night? What would you do if you heard her screaming and begging him to stop hurting her?" I asked.

Craig stopped walking, and without intending to, I did too.

I couldn't really see him properly but I could see enough to know that he was looking at me in a sad way.

"Dawn, you're a very strong girl to be able to stand up to a bully like your Dad. What you did couldn't have been easy, but sometimes it takes police and social work a lot of time to be able to get something like this fixed."

"What do you mean 'fixed'? They can't fix it. They told me I've got to go back home. That's not fixed, that's living it all over again, except it's going to be much worse this time as he'll be mad and I'll get it, Danny will get it and Mum will get it even worse" I said.

Nobody could help me, I thought, this was as bad as it could get. But I will tell you this if he dares put one finger on Danny he'll be sorry, I swear he will, I thought to myself.

"Dawn, this may sound like hard advice to take in, but if you just give it time, then they'll sort it out. I promise you they'll not let your Dad away without watching him closely" Craig said.

"But how can they watch him? They can't move into our house, so they can't help."

"Dawn, it is a little complicated to understand, so let's just say that to ensure a child gets all they need, sometimes lots of different adults get together to make sure that happens. These adults can be teachers, doctors, police, social workers and anybody else that may be able to help that child. They meet on a regular basis and agree on what each person can do to help that child, then when they meet again they make sure those things have happened. Now, the child's parents have to go to those meetings too. This means that the parents will know that everyone is watching the family very closely. In your case it will also give your Mum confidence that there are many people who she can speak to, to get help."

"What do you mean they get all they need? You mean like toys?" I asked

"Not quite. All children have the right to grow up safely in the world and there are lots of things we can do to do to make sure that we get it right for every child. We need to make sure they are safe, healthy, achieving, nurtured, active, respected, responsible and included in the community. If any of these things are not being done, then that's when those meetings happen. That's a big long list of things that probably don't even make sense to you, but it's a list that adults use to make sure they don't miss anything. It sounds like a lot to take in, but all you need to know is that there will be lots of people meeting to make sure that you and Danny are safe. You will also have someone you can go to – Margaret – if you need to speak about anything that may be bothering you." Craig said in a way that I understood.

That was the second time I'd heard someone say that things happen for a reason, so maybe that bit was true and they may hold meetings to make sure we are safe, but who's gonna watch Dad and stop him when he's in the middle of beating us up? He's not going to do that at a meeting. I was scared, tired and so lonely. I just wanted to go to the WOL and live there forever. *Please, Mirabriel, just take me there to live forever.*

All of a sudden a bright light sparkled just to my right and Mirabriel giggled in my ear as she stood on my shoulder. She quickly reminded me not to say a word as Craig could not see or hear her.

I looked over at Craig and he was carrying on as normal, he really hadn't noticed her. That light was so bright, how on earth was she not seen by the whole world I wondered.

Craig's dog started barking for no reason.

"Animals are so sensitive that they can sense me," Mirabriel chuckled, "But he can't exactly tell anyone what he is seeing, can he?!" she finished.

"Wow, that's amazing." I said

"What is?" Craig asked

"Oh nothing, I just think it's great that Buddy stops barking when you tell him. What kind of dog is he?" I asked in a rush to change the subject so he didn't realise that I was talking to my invisible friend!

"He's a springer spaniel" he replied.

"Cool."

Mirabriel was speaking to me at the same time as Craig and I was able to make out what both were saying. I was quite impressed with myself.

"Dawn, my dear sweet child I know this is hard for you but please trust. Trust that there is a very good reason that this is happening," Mirabriel said in the gentle caring way that she always did.

"Why do I keep hearing that?" I asked, remembering to ask her through my thoughts so Craig didn't hear me speaking to her.

"Because in life everything is not always as it may seem, just remember the story about the hole in the wall" she said. "If you remember that for everything you go through in life, it will help you during difficult times."

I didn't really understand what she meant, but I trusted her and I guessed if it gave me something positive to focus on then it should be able to help me.

"Are you ok Dawn?" Craig asked, very loudly.

I was suddenly aware that he had been speaking to me but I hadn't responded. I had been too busy trying to work out why I no longer felt scared.

"Because, my dear sweet child you have your guardian Frangel – me - right by your side." Mirabriel said. "Your guardian Frangel is your protector and will not let any real harm come to you. They allow lessons to be learnt, which may cause you to experience some things in life that are hard to cope with, but they will always be by your side to help you muddle through. Even if you can't see the positive reason for it at the time, you will see in time to come. You just need to trust, trust in them and trust in yourself and trust in me, your guardian Frangel - Mirabriel. Trust we will never leave you my dear sweet Dawn, we love you so very much" and with that she vanished.

"Dawn, are you alright?" Craig asked again.

"Oh errrmmm yes," I replied. I was still a bit dazed trying to take everything in whilst also trying to work out why I had such conflicting feelings of fear and trust at the same time. Just a few hours ago I had trusted, yet they'd let me down, they were sending me home. Yet for some reason here I was trusting again. It didn't make sense, yet it felt right.

"Dawn, I know how hard this must be for you and I think you're incredibly brave. I have a daughter who's the same age as you and I can't imagine her having to go through what you are," Craig said. "You're a good role model to others, you can teach them how to be strong and you don't even realise you do it."

I was taken aback. "Really? I don't see why anybody would want to be like me," I said quietly.

"Because what you did took more bravery and strength than many adults have and now you're going to go back home and be strong again knowing everything will work out eventually. That makes you the kind of brave, strong person so many people would love to be" he said.

As Craig was talking we continued walking and I was listening so intently that I wasn't aware we'd been walking until I saw the street lights.

"Wait! Stop!" I panicked. Craig and Buddy both stopped and looked at me. "What's going to happen to me now?" I asked.

"I'm taking you back to Margaret who's going to take you back home," he replied.

I looked at Buddy and started to cry. "Could I give Buddy a hug, please?" I asked.

"Of course you can," Craig said.

I went onto my knees and before I even called his name Buddy came over to me and put his head near mine, licking my face. I giggled then I cried some more. I wasn't sure why I felt so close to Buddy but knowing I could have died in the cold without him finding me made him very special and I think he knew that. I sat hugging him for a few minutes as I heard voices getting closer. I whispered into his ear, "Thank you for finding me Buddy, I can go home and look after my brother and my Mum now." As I held onto his neck, he licked my tears away, as if he knew exactly what I was saying.

I stood up as I heard Margaret's voice "Dawn!" as she was running towards me, looking upset yet happy at the same time. She ran up to me and hugged me tighter than I had ever been hugged before.

"Dawn, oh Dawn, I've been so worried about you," she said with tears rolling down her cheeks. "Thank the Frangels you're alright."

I looked up at her. "You mean you believe in Frangels too?" I asked in amazement.

She kept me close to her and said, "I prayed to them to keep you safe as soon as I heard that you'd run away. You're here safe now. Of course I believe in them. Just because you can't see them doesn't mean they don't exist. They certainly do and as soon as I get a quiet moment I'll be thanking them for keeping you safe." I'd never known so much care, I was used to nobody caring.

I saw the bull nose lady and the Mary lady walking towards us "We've been so worried about you, Dawn," the Mary lady said as she stood next to me and put her arm on my shoulder.

"Yes we have, very worried indeed," the bull nose lady said ruffling my hair.

Wow, why are all these people here caring about me? Me? Why care about me? I thought. And without even seeing Mirabriel I heard her voice.

"Perhaps this is one of the reasons things have gone as they have. So you could see that there really are people who do care about you. You are a special little girl. You need to see how strong you are because you are so much stronger than you think. I love you, my precious sweet child, and I will never leave you. I am here even when you cannot see, hear or feel me."

I looked around and saw many people who cared. It was the first time in my life that I'd really felt it and it was a nice feeling.

"Do I still have to go home?" I asked.

The bull nose lady put her hand on my shoulder but before she could speak Margaret crouched down so she was at my height.

"Dawn, yes you do, my darling, but I promise you that I am going to see you in school every week to spend some time with you. Police and social work will be having meetings often to make sure this doesn't happen again," she reassured me.

I looked in her eyes as she spoke to me and I believed her.

"Are you my guardian Frangel?" I asked her.

She looked at me with watery eyes and said, "No, but I will do the same job as your guardian Frangel, so you then have two of us looking after you." She smiled.

"I believe you," I said and she hugged me.

"Come on, let's get you home," she said.

As we walked away I noticed Craig and Buddy walking down the path after us. I ran back towards them and wrapped my arms around Craig's waist.

"Thank you for being so nice and for helping me!"

"Hey, kid, you're a brave girl, and I meant it when I said that if you were my daughter I'd be very proud of you." Craig patted my back.

"And thank you, Buddy, I love you!" I said as I hugged him before running back to the others.

We got to the path at the end of the lane and that's when I realised we were back at the house that I ran away from.

"Wow, did Buddy follow me all the way from here?" I asked out loud.

Craig chuckled from behind me. "Yes, he did, he followed your scent all the way from here."

I could see the police van on the road in front of the house.

"Can I give him a treat?" I asked.

"Sure, kid" Craig said and he handed me Buddy's ball.

Buddy got very excited as he waited for me to throw it. I threw it down the lane and he ran after it with his tail wagging, I giggled as I watched him.

Margaret came with me in the car and my journey home began. The bull nose lady was driving and the Mary lady was in the other seat in the front. Margaret and I sat in the back.

The journey home was very quiet, nobody really said much other than to tell me I would be okay and that I'd done really well today. Well, it sure didn't feel like it. The sick feeling in my tummy sure didn't make me feel that I'd be okay either.

I could see the house getting closer and I thought I was going to be sick. I just wanted to run away again. But with these three beside me I had no chance and I knew they knew it.

"You don't need to be afraid. I'm right here by your side." It was Mirabriel and although I couldn't see her, her voice and words always seemed to make me feel better. Knowing she really was there helped so much, it was reassuring. I knew she wouldn't lie to me and I knew if she said she would be there then that is what she would do. I trusted her.

As the car stopped Margaret told me she'd see me next week and if I wanted to speak to her before then all I had to do was to ask my teacher to call her. She said my Mum and Dad wouldn't know if my teacher called her, which made me feel better.

I looked over to the house and saw the lights on inside.

"I'm with you," Mirabriel said. "Remember your calm breathing. Breathe into your tummy until you count to five, then hold it and count to five and let it out counting to five" she reminded me.

I did what she said and the sick feeling went away. But it came back as soon as I stopped.

"Keep doing it," she said

"You mean you know what I'm feeling?" I asked aloud.

"We understand how difficult this must be for you, Dawn, but we won't leave you in the house until we're happy that you're going to be okay," the bull nose lady said.

Phew, that had been close! I forgot again I thought as I heard Mirabriel chuckle in my ear.

"Thank you" was all I could manage.

"Remember your breathing."

CHAPTER FOURTEEN

I don't know how I did it, but somehow I managed to get myself out of the car. I kept breathing the way Mirabriel had told me to, which did help me feel calm, but it wasn't easy to remember to keep doing it. Mirabriel shouted "Breathe!" every time I forgot. At one point I actually giggled when she shouted. The bull nose lady noticed and told me that it was nice to see me laughing and she was glad I was feeling better.

She had no idea that I have never felt so bad about anything in my life as I felt at the thought of walking through that door. I knew I just had to get on with it and with Mirabriel next to me it made me feel much better, even if she did yell "Breathe" every two minutes. It made me feel as if I was slipping into a suit of armour that protected me and helped me cope with anything, so I was happy to be reminded to do the breathing thing.

As soon as I got out of the car I saw Mum and Danny come out of the house. Danny ran as fast as his little legs would let him. He ran straight into me and put his arms around my waist and hugged me so tight that I thought he was going to squeeze my dinner out of me. I was surprised at his reaction. Sure, I knew

Dan loved me, but hey, he's a boy and he likes to think he's all macho.

"Dawn, I was scared you were never coming home again," he said.

I couldn't speak because when I looked up I saw Mum walking towards me, but Dad was just standing at the door, looking. Just looking. Saying nothing and not moving, just looking.

"Breathe," I heard the voice shout.

I was struggling to remember what breathe meant as my heart raced not knowing what was coming when that front door closed with all of us on the other side of it. Where were they going to be? Safe in their own beds. They weren't going to get a beating or have to hear their Mum getting it instead.

Mum came up to me and I could see the tears in her eyes. She hugged me so tight that I thought I was going to be sick. She held my face in her hands and looked into my eyes as she told me that she was sorry.

Sorry? I'd just gone against my family, telling social work and police what went on in our house and then I ran away and she tells me that *she* is sorry?! Well that definitely wasn't the reaction I'd been expecting that's for sure.

Out of the corner of my eye I saw Dad walking towards me. My tummy nearly leapt out of my body. I felt so sick. But as he got closer I saw something in his eyes that I'd never seen before. I can't explain what it was, but they didn't have that mad angry look in them that he normally had. He came over to me and put his arm around me. The first thing I noticed was that he didn't smell of drink. This was all very confusing but I wasn't complaining. It was weird as Dad almost had a gentleness about him. So many thoughts were going around my head all at once.

Dad thanked the Mary lady for finding me, telling her they had all been very worried about me. He was so false he made me sick.

Danny grabbed my hand and pulled me towards the house. I pulled away and ran over to Margaret who was standing with the bull nose lady and Mary lady. I gave her the biggest hug that I think I have ever given anyone in my life. After I'd done it I thought that I shouldn't have, but she squeezed me tight and stroked my hair and told me I'd be okay. She said she was proud of me so I knew it was okay. Then I ran over to Danny as Mum and Dad were talking to the Mary lady and bull nose lady.

Danny and I went into the house. As soon as we got in he asked me about ten questions all one after the other.

"Whoa, wait Dan," I said, "I can't keep up with all your questions to actually answer any of them for you. What is Dad going to say when he gets in?" I asked feeling panicky

"Breathe!" came my timely reminder.

"Hey, Mirabriel, I heard you but I can't see you, are you really there?" Danny asked.

I forgot Danny could hear her too. "Never mind that," I interrupted, "Is Dad going to go mad on me?"

"Dawn, I've never seen him look so worried or scared." Danny replied. "He was constantly phoning the police to see if you had been found. Anyway, where were you? Where did you go? Why did you run away? Why?" he asked.

"Stop!" I interrupted again. "Danny. I'll tell you later when Mum and Dad are out of the way."

At that point I heard a car drive away and as I looked out of the window I saw the bull nose lady's car drive away from our house. That's it then, they're gone. My safety and protection are gone. I saw Mum and Dad walking down the path and I felt sick again.

"Breathe."

"Why do you keep telling her to breathe Mirabriel? Of course she's breathing, she'd be dead if she wasn't," came Danny's curious voice.

"Danny, shoosht" I said quickly just as Mum and Dad walked into the house.

I didn't know what to do or what to say. I was scared, so I just concentrated on breathing the same way Mirabriel did. Concentrating on my breathing seemed to make me feel much calmer and I wanted to keep focussing on it to keep that feeling. Which meant I wasn't thinking of what was about to happen. I headed towards my bedroom when Dad called me back and I braced myself for what was to come. *Here we go* I thought. I knew it wouldn't take long before he started. I wondered if the bull nose lady had even got to the end of the road as here he was starting already, just like I told her he would!

I went back into the living room and before I sat down or even looked at him all I heard was, "I'm sorry, Dawn."

My head shot up and I looked at him. Did I just hear right? Dad looked at me as he walked over to where I was standing. He put both his hands on my shoulders "I have been so wrong in all I've done, Dawn, and I am so sorry," he said.

Well, that's the very last thing I expected. Was it a trick I wondered? Is he just trying to reel me in so he can get closer to hit me? But it never came. It didn't happen. He hugged me tight and told me that he was sorry about five times.

"Dawn, what I did was wrong, I know it was wrong and I'm so sorry. Sometimes I react badly when I know I shouldn't and I'm sorry."

I was so taken aback. It certainly wasn't the reaction I'd expected from him. I never said anything, I couldn't say anything.

After a few minutes of silence and him hugging me, he stood back, holding both my shoulders as he looked at me and said, "Dawn, things are going to be very different around here from now on, I promise." He said in such a convincing way that I actually believed him.

I didn't know what to say and all I could manage was, "Dad, I'm so tired can I go to bed?" He nodded and I went upstairs to my room. I walked past Mum and never said anything.

I got into my room and flopped onto my bed. I was so tired, but also confused and relieved, yet still scared.

I wasn't long in my room when Danny came in. He was full of questions and asked so many that I couldn't answer one as he was too busy asking another.

I told him what happened and asked him what had happened at home. He told me that Mum and Dad had a huge argument and Mum had been the one doing the shouting, telling him that everything was his fault because of the way he treated us. He said that he had never heard Mum speak to Dad that way before but she was proper mad with him.

"What did Dad do?" I asked.

"Nothing, that was what was so strange. I expected him to go mad and I thought she would end up in hospital but he just sat down with his head in his hands crying," Dan said.

"Crying!" I exclaimed.

"Yes, he cried and kept saying how sorry he was and how none of this was meant to happen this way."

I couldn't believe what I was hearing. I was so shocked to hear that Mum had actually stood up to Dad like that. That was a very brave thing to do, I thought. Then Danny told me they'd interviewed him in school too.

"What did you tell them?"

He hung his head down and started to cry. "Nothing. I said nothing and I'm sorry because I know I let you down by not telling the truth," he said.

"But Danny, if you'd told them the truth we would have been taken away from this place. Why didn't you tell them?" I asked, frustrated. "I did what I did today to save us for nothing, because you never said anything."

"Dawn, I was too scared when they asked me questions. I really wanted to tell them and I nearly did, but all I could hear was Mum and Dad telling me that I'd never be believed and then I'd get it when I got home. I couldn't say anything, I just couldn't. I was too scared, I'm sorry," he said as the tears rolled down his face.

"Danny, it's okay, really it is. Mirabriel told me everything happens for a reason. Craig told me everything happens for a reason. I trust them both, so I trust there's a good reason for this too, even if we can't see what it is right now, I know we will in time. Maybe this is what had to happen to make Mum stick up for herself and for us and at least we know that we can go to tell someone and we will be believed. So please don't worry, okay?" I put my hand on his arm. I was surprised at how calm I felt after what he'd told me. I thought I'd be mad but I kept hearing everything Craig, Margaret and Mirabriel told me today.

Danny stopped crying and looked at me. "Who's Craig?"

"He's the policeman who owns Buddy, the police dog who found me when I was lost in the dark," I said with a smile that I couldn't shift.

"Gee, Dawn, you sure know how to have fun!" Danny laughed.

We chatted for what seemed like ages as I answered Danny's stream of questions, but I was getting sleepy, it had been a long day.

"Yes, you do need to rest, my sweet child Dawn," came the voice in my ear.

"Thank you, Mirabriel, and thank you for being with me today," I said.

"Why are you talking to Mirabriel when you can't see her?" Danny asked.

"I don't need to see her anymore, I can hear her speak to me without seeing her, Dan. All I need to do is trust that she is with me, even if she doesn't answer me back. I know she hears me and is protecting me."

"Yeah, right!" Danny said disbelievingly.

"Okay, I'll prove it – I'll speak to Mirabriel and ask her to appear when I get to the count of ten."

"Okay, but she always comes when you call her," Danny said still disbelieving me.

"Yeah, and that's why I'm counting to ten to show you she hears what I'm saying. Ready?"

"Sure," Danny said still not believing me. "I know she'll appear straight away when you call her name, she always does."

"Okay, to prove she hears me now then I'll count to ten but I won't use her name. That way you'll know she must be with me."

"One… two… three…" I started counting

Danny was looking at me as if I was mad.

"Four… five… six… seven… eight… nine… ten!" I finished.

As soon as I said ten the familiar burst of bright white light appeared with an abundance of rainbow stars and Mirabriel jumped out of the middle of it.

"Well, well, Danny, my sweet child, I do hear you and I heard you disbelieving Dawn. All you've got to do is believe that your Frangel is with you and trust that he or she will be there. Even if you can't see them, they will be there." she said in her usual sweet voice.

"Wow!" Danny managed to squeak.

Mirabriel and I giggled. Just then my bedroom door opened and my Mum came in. Mirabriel managed to disappear within a second so Mum didn't see her, Mirabriel was good at that I thought to myself.

Mum looked more scared than before, yet Dad was so calm. I'd never seen Dad that calm when he had reason to be angry. It unnerved me and I didn't like it.

CHAPTER FIFTEEN

She sat on the edge of my bed and smiled with tears rolling down her face. I didn't know what I was meant to say, I felt very uneasy.

"What is it, Mum?" I asked quietly. "What's he done? Are you being punished for what I did?" I asked nervously.

"No, no he hasn't done anything, Dawn. I'm just so relieved that you're home. I was really worried about you." She dried the tears from her eyes.

"I'm... I'm really sorry Mum, but I couldn't take it anymore," I said holding back my tears. Mum looked at the floor as if she didn't know what to say to me.

Did she feel guilty? Did she hate me? Did she wish I'd never come back? I had so many thoughts running through my head.

"Dawn, none of this is your fault, you shouldn't have to put up with all that you do. It's my fault, I shouldn't let you see what you see and I should protect you more often than I do." Mum said.

"No, Mum, it's not your fault," I said. I went up to her and put my arms out to hug her. She didn't really hug me back properly. I didn't know if that was

151

because what I did was wrong or because she really hated me.

"She doesn't hate you my dear sweet child, she feels guilty for not being able to protect you and she doesn't know how to cope with that guilt" came Mirabriel's reassuring voice.

I was getting much better at speaking to Mirabriel through my thoughts and I started telling her that it felt like my Mum really did hate me.

"Dawn, my sweet child, look at her. Those tears are tears of pain. Pain because she hurts knowing that she is unable to protect you. All of this is going to be making you, your Mum and Danny grow stronger every day, you just won't realise it for some time yet."

I knew that Mirabriel was trying to make me feel better but I also knew that she was right. I don't know how I knew, but somehow I just did.

"Of course you just know," the familiar voice said. "Don't you ever get a feeling that something is or is not right? When you get that feeling, you need to trust it. Some people call it a 'gut instinct' or a 'gut feeling,' because it's a feeling in your tummy that feels strong. That is what you need to learn to trust and listen to that feeling."

I looked at Danny who appeared to be deep in thought, smiling, as if he understood every word. He looked very much at peace within himself.

Mum was still sitting on the bed looking at the floor then to me and Danny then back to the floor. It was as if she didn't know what to say or do. I felt like I needed to give her another hug but I wasn't sure if it was the right thing to do.

"Trust your feelings," came the familiar voice.

I went over to Mum on the bed and without saying anything I just put my arms around her and hugged her. She hugged me back so tight I thought she was going to squeeze me to death as she was stroking my hair telling me how sorry she was. I opened my eyes and saw Danny sitting looking at us. I waved my arm to tell him to come over, as he did Mum and I both put our arms around him and the three of us just hugged for what seemed like ages. It was the first time I could remember feeling safe with Mum.

Suddenly the bedroom door flew open and Dad appeared at the door. He never said anything, but he didn't need to for all three of us to jump in fright. Dad spent a few minutes just looking at us all, saying nothing. Not a word. But he didn't need to. I knew that look in his eyes. He was mad. This must be the fear feeling in my tummy Mirabriel told me about. I knew that Mum and Danny felt it too as they sat in silence. All six eyes staring at Dad in fearful anticipation as he stood in the doorway.

"Is everything okay?" Dad asked in that voice, the voice which we all knew and feared. He's not capable of being nice to us for very long, he seemed to thrive on making us miserable.

"I'm coming. Right, come on you two get ready for bed," Mum said in panic, with the tone that suggested she knew Dad's mood.

"It's okay, just leave them alone," Dad said. If he didn't have that look in his eyes I'd have thought he meant it, but I knew underneath those words was a man who was mad and angry. I knew when he saw us all hugging that it would set him off – he never liked Mum giving us attention. I used to hear Mum tell her friends that he was jealous of us. But they were the days when she actually had more than one friend.

When I was little, Mum used to visit friends and have coffee whilst I played with their kids. But she doesn't see her friends anymore. Dad used to give her a hard time each time she went, I'd hear him shouting at her that she wasn't being a good wife and she should've been at home looking after the house or being a good mother. I could never understand why he said that, as she *was* a good Mum. She made me happy but the more he got on at her the less we went to see her friends, until she never went to see them at all. Apart from just one friend who she never saw much, but when she did see her she spent most of her time trying to persuade Mum to leave Dad. I was sad for Mum because when she was with her friends she always seemed very happy. I used to think that maybe Dad was right and she must've been a bad wife, but as I have got older I could see that she was always doing stuff for him and for us. I don't know why he still says that but I don't really know what a wife is meant to do. The one thing I was sure of was that I wanted her to be happy like she was when she was with her friends, but I want her to be like that all the time. Maybe you're not meant to be happy when you are a wife. If that is true then I never want to be anybody's wife, not ever!

I'd watched films on the television though, where families were happy, including the wife of the family. This grown up stuff really confused me. Maybe I'd prefer to just never grow up, I thought to myself.

Dad came into the room and put his arms around me and told Danny and Mum to cuddle in too. This was confusing because I could feel that he was proper mad, I sensed his angry energy, but if he really was in a mood then why would he hug us. I had no idea, he never made any sense to me. I'll just not think about it and make the most of it while he's being nice to us. After he pulled us all together he told us he loved us and he was sorry. He didn't seem as mad, maybe I was just afraid and he wasn't mad at all. I felt so tired that I wanted them all to get out of my room and leave me alone. With that thought, Dad said that they should all go and let me get some sleep as it had been a long day for me.

Mum kissed my forehead and said goodnight. Danny gave me a high five and ruffled my hair and said, "Good night sis, I'm so glad you're home."

That left Dad and me. I felt sick, I had no idea what was coming. He sat on the edge of my bed and told me that he was sorry, he knew what he did was wrong and he wouldn't let that happen again. But then leaning into me he told me in a quiet whispered voice that he warned me before never to tell anyone and I should listen to him in future. He ruffled my hair and said good night. It was as if he was being friendly but with anger which at that moment he seemed able to control. When he left the room I got into bed in my clothes. I was too tired to change. I lay with my head on my pillow and I cried and cried and cried. I didn't think I had any tears left to cry but, oh boy, I did. They just wouldn't stop falling. I felt so scared of Dad. He was even more unpredictable than normal and I just didn't know how to take him. He was right about one thing though, I really should have listened to him because nobody believed me.

I sobbed into my pillow so nobody could hear me crying. If Dad heard me that would probably make him really mad and he may not be able to hide it this time, I felt so sad. Earlier that day I really believed that I would be going somewhere safe, yet here I was back in this stupid house.

I was starting to feel angry again that nobody believed me. As I felt the anger building up inside me a familiar burst of white light shone and rainbow stars appeared on my pillow. As always, when I really needed her I forgot to ask for her help, but she obviously knew I needed it and she appeared anyway.

"Now, now, Dawn my sweet child, have you really forgotten all that's been said today?"

"Yes I have. I hate it here. I hate everyone. I hate everything. Why does my life have to be like this?" I asked in between sobs.

"Dawn, I know you are hurting and I know it's because you don't know what your Dad is going to do and not knowing is often so much worse than actually being aware of what's happening," she said "That's what makes it so difficult to cope with."

I couldn't say anything. I was sad, confused, angry and didn't know what to think anymore.

"Dawn, just remember what we spoke about earlier. Everything does happen for a reason and even though you can't see the reason you just need to trust."

"Yes but you heard Dad – he told me I'd never be believed and he was right."

"Dawn, your Dad has a big influence in what you believe because you have grown up believing that he is being honest with you. You have grown up trusting him because that's just what kids do, but your Dad is not always right and you shouldn't believe everything he tells you. He is looking out for himself. He knows that he was very close to being caught today so he wants to make sure he never gets that close to being caught again and the only way he can do that is to tell you that you won't be believed to stop you from telling anybody again." Mirabriel said this with so much certainty that I knew she meant it.

I remembered everything that I'd been told about not having enough evidence and that's why they couldn't take me away. I thought about Margaret and Craig who really seemed to care and everything they told me made sense to me, so I guess I had to trust.

As the sun burst through my bedroom curtains I forgot where I was, what day it was or even if I had school. I got up and went to the bathroom and could smell cooking downstairs. That never happened so I knew it wasn't for Danny or me. Mum never made us breakfast and Dad certainly didn't. If there were any bananas in the house that's the most we got and even that was on a good day.

I went back to bed and pulled the covers over my head. I didn't really care if it was a school day. I was happy to hide underneath my duvet. I started to speak to Mirabriel through my thoughts when I heard footsteps on the stairs. I closed my eyes and pretended to be asleep. I didn't really want to speak to anybody.

CHAPTER SIXTEEN

"Come on Dawn, your Ready Brek is waiting," Mum shouted. I didn't even know what Ready Brek was, I'd never heard of it. I pretended I was asleep and didn't answer. Mum came upstairs and I was aware of her standing in my room. I stayed quiet until she lifted the covers from my head and stood over me. I peeked one eye open and realised she actually looked happy, which didn't happen very often.

"Where's Dad?" I asked, expecting her to tell me that he was still in bed.

"He's making your breakfast," came her unexpected reply.

"Breakfast?" I repeated. I failed in my search for words as panic set in. If Dad was making breakfast, then he'd be mad if we weren't there to eat it. I pushed past Mum to get to the bathroom.

"Oi! What's got into you?" Mum asked.

"Nothing, I just don't want to be late." I replied fearfully as I ran into Dan's bedroom to make sure he was up, telling him to get dressed quickly and get downstairs.

I was getting ready for school and I kept telling myself to make sure I looked grateful as I ate whatever that stuff was that Dad was making. I felt sick already, not knowing what he was up to and why he was making us breakfast. Was he trying to pretend he was kind? Or that he cared? Maybe he was going to poison us. He'd never even shopped for breakfast let alone actually got out of bed to make it. I felt very uneasy.

"Breathe," came a familiar voice.

"I… can't see you Mirabriel. Let me see you, please. I need to know you are there," I begged.

"Now Dawn, stop that right now. You don't need to see me to know I'm here, you can hear me perfectly well. Now focus on your breathing and the sick feeling won't feel so bad," she reminded me "your thoughts are stressing you."

I knew she was right - the breathing thing did make me feel better each time I did it. Even just one deep breath made me feel better.

"Yes, it would have, my child, but don't stop at just one breath," Mirabriel said.

"Grrr! Sometimes it's really annoying that you can hear my thoughts, you know. Can't I have any privacy around here?" I snapped.

Mirabriel appeared and stuck out her tongue as she pointed at me and lots of brightly coloured rainbow stars fell around us. "Now young lady, just you listen up. I am here to help you, but how am I meant to do that if I don't know what's going on in that head of yours?"

I knew she was right. Anytime Mirabriel heard my negative thoughts she showed me how to turn them into a positive. Mirabriel looked at me and smiled, she didn't have to say anything. I knew she heard me and her smile told me that she knew I didn't really mean to get mad with her.

All these distractions helped me forget that I was going downstairs to Dad. My feet were on the last step when I looked into the kitchen and saw him. My heart felt like it was going to leap out of my chest.

Dad was dressed, he'd even shaved and he was singing as he put two bowls of steaming white gooey stuff on the table. He put his arm around me and smiled. He was so strangely calm it was almost eerie.

"Good morning," he said. "Here you go, Dawn, a good healthy breakfast to fill you both up before you go to school." He pulled out a chair at the kitchen table for me. He must have tidied it up. I've never seen that table without washing on it and I've never seen Dad tidy anything away. He leaves his stuff lying around and either shouts at Mum to come and do it for him or he just leaves it where it is.

"Ah, good morning Dan, my son, you're just in time. Come and sit down." Dad said as he pulled a chair out for him. Dan gave me a confused and afraid stare. It was unnerving to see Dad like this, it was like someone standing with a balloon and a pin, waiting for it to burst. I looked away quickly to avoid Dad seeing our expressions of confusion and fear.

I looked at my plate. What was this gunk? It looked like wallpaper paste. But I had to eat it, if I didn't I knew what would come next and it wouldn't be pleasant.

I ate a spoonful and actually enjoyed it. It was warm and tasty. I must have eaten the rest of my bowl like it was about to be stolen from me because when I'd finished I looked up and Dad was staring at me. Oh no, had I eaten it too quickly? Was I not meant to eat it all? I felt sick and started to panic. What was coming now? Was I in for it again? I looked at Dan and he was nearly finished his bowl too. Oh no Dan, slow down, please, I thought to myself.

"Well, guys, you must have enjoyed that!" Dad said, smiling as I felt my body sink into the chair with relief. He wasn't mad at us.

My tummy felt strange. I'd never really felt like this before - full up with no room to eat anything else. Normally after we'd had a meal at home we would still be hungry, this feeling of being full up was very strange indeed. But I liked it and Danny looked equally satisfied.

"Right, you two, go get your bags and I'll take you to school," Dad said.

Danny and I shot each other a look. What was going on? Never in our lives had Dad ever given us a lift to school, not even when it had been snowing. Whatever was going on I didn't understand it, nor did I like it, but I also knew not to argue.

Danny and I grabbed our bags and got into the car but because Dad was there we couldn't say anything to each other. I assumed by Danny's face that he was trying as hard as I was to work out what was going on.

As we drove to school Dad put the radio on and sang along to one of the songs. I had no idea what had got into him. He stopped the car at the school gates and lots of people were looking at us. Dad told us to have a good day and to just get the bus home as normal after school. We got out of the car and walked towards the gates to the sound of people giggling and muttering, I couldn't hear what was being said but I knew it was about us.

"There's pee pants!" a voice I didn't recognise said.

"Oooohhh, Daddy's giving them a lift to school!" said another voice.

"Yeah, Daddy drunk," said another boy, pretending to be drunk and falling over as he said it.

I was so embarrassed, I wanted to die right there.

Why did my life have to be so different? Why couldn't I be like normal children? I looked around and there were people playing football, tig and hopscotch. Others were standing chatting or laughing. They all looked happy as if they didn't really have anything to worry about. As I watched them I wondered what it must be like to live their lives. I couldn't imagine what it would be like to be happy and not to worry about what was going to happen when I went home every night. I felt a lump in my throat as I wished I could be like them. What did I do that was so bad to deserve my kind of life? Was it my fault? Was I such a bad person?

So many thoughts were going through my head at once when suddenly I felt something around my ankle and before I could look to see what it was I was lying flat on my face with blood pouring from my nose. People formed a circle around me laughing and pointing. I couldn't see Danny so he must have gone to his friends before I had fallen. I was so embarrassed, I didn't know what to say or do, so I just put my head on the ground and lay there. I could hear people calling me different nasty names.

Why me? What had I done to deserve this? I'd never hurt anybody. I'd never called anybody a name that made them feel bad, so why did they pick on me? I didn't understand.

Everything went white in front of me and all I could see was a thistle that looked like a house.

"Tonight I'll bring you here and teach you how to dream walk, which will help you cope with bullies" Frangel Briadh said. I couldn't see her, I could only hear her. But I knew it was her for sure.

The next voice I heard was Mr Mackintosh's, the head teacher, who lifted me up off the ground and told everyone else that he wanted to see them in his office at 9 o'clock.

The nurse cleaned the blood from me in the same room I'd sat in for hours the day before.

"Bringing back memories, huh?" she said as if she could read my thoughts.

Yes, I thought to myself, it was indeed. Memories that left me confused. I'd expected to be in so much trouble when I'd gone home after the last time I'd been in here, but I hadn't. Dad had quiet words with me and left me afraid that something was coming my way, but I'd got up the next day and he'd been singing, making breakfast and took us to school! All things he'd never done before. I couldn't work it out. The nurse saw that I was lost in my thoughts.

"How are things at home, Dawn?" she asked. I didn't mind telling her as she seemed to genuinely care. But then they all did and look where that had got me.

"Why is my life so different from all the other kids?" I asked.

She put her hand on my shoulder, "In what way, Dawn?"

"Well, they all seem so carefree, like they never have anything to worry about." It was true. I was so different from them and they knew it too. That's why they are nasty to me and Danny.

"Dawn, you're such a beautiful child and so much wiser and stronger than you'll ever realise. You may have more worries than other children but you have much more strength, love and patience too" the nurse replied. That didn't really tell me why I was so different, but I didn't want to say anymore in case she probed for more information so I just smiled.

After she'd finished cleaning me up I went back to class. I was dreading walking into the room. My tummy was in knots and I felt sick as I knew they were going to make fun of me.

"Breathe," instructed Mirabriel's familiar voice. "Come on, you need to practice all the time so it becomes automatic, you know it helps you."

I knew she was right, but it didn't stop me feeling annoyed every time she reminded me. I started counting my breaths and, as always, I felt much calmer.....nervous......but calmer. I got to the classroom door whilst counting my breaths. I knocked, then opened it and I felt every pair of eyes in the room staring at me. At first nobody said anything but then the giggles started and I saw people whispering to each other. Some even pointed at me as they muttered to each other quietly.

The teacher looked at me with pity.

"Sheeeesht," she told the class, but nobody paid any attention to her. They carried on sniggering and pointing. All of a sudden I felt angry. If only they had to live a day in my life they wouldn't be laughing. They had no idea how lucky they were I thought to myself.

"Tell them," Mirabriel said in a firm tone I'd never heard her use.

"Dawn tell them, tell them how their actions make you feel. If you don't tell them they will never understand," she continued in the same serious tone.

"But they won't understand! And even if they did they wouldn't care. Why would they be so unkind if they cared? There's no point" I replied through my thoughts as I started to walk back to my seat.

"Tell them!" she repeated, with even more determination. I ignored her and kept walking towards my seat.

"They need to know, Dawn, now stop where you are and tell them."

"No!" I replied firmly. "I won't. They don't care and I'll only end up making a fool of myself which will give them more reason to make fun of me."

"Tell them!" She wasn't giving up. "I am with you."

I had no intention of telling anybody anything, but just as I had almost reached my seat, fighting the tears back, I heard someone laugh as they put their foot out to trip me up.

"Ha ha, enjoy your trip," I heard them say.

"Tell them NOW, Dawn!" Mirabriel said.

As she spoke I found myself walking away from the foot that was going to trip me up and towards the front of the class. I heard more giggles and a few people muttering that I was a coward. Everything around me became a blur, all I could see was the blackboard. I've no idea where it came from, but I was suddenly filled with a mixture of anger and strength.

"I am with you, Dawn. You can't see me but you know I am right on your shoulder. You can do this – they need to know." Mirabriel said.

I got to the blackboard and the teacher went to speak to me.

I put my hand up to stop her and said, "Please Miss, let me have just one minute to speak."

CHAPTER SEVENTEEN

The class went silent and I felt every pair of eyes burning holes in me. The teacher stood still, she obviously had no idea what I was about to do. I was the quiet one in class who just came in, did my work and went home. But at that moment I really didn't care, I had a strength in me that I'd never felt before and I was determined to use it.

I stopped in front of the blackboard in the centre of the room and focused on the class. I can't explain what I felt but I knew Mirabriel was with me and that made me feel at peace without losing the strength I needed. Before I said anything I looked at everyone in the room. Nobody was laughing. Nobody was speaking. For the first time in my life I felt I had the tiniest bit of control over what I was doing. Mirabriel was right, they did need to know and unless I told them they wouldn't be aware of how they made me feel.

"Why do you feel the need to make someone sad?" I asked nobody in particular, casting my eyes over the entire class. Nobody said a word. "Why do you have to make someone hurt more than they hurt already?"

"Why do you have to make the only safe place in the world for me a place I no longer feel safe?" I continued in a strong and determined voice. Still nobody spoke. The class was silent and instead of staring at me they all stared at the floor. This gave me more strength. I wasn't going to let them bully me the way they did without saying all I had to say.

"Do you have any idea what goes on in my life? How much I need to come to school to feel safe? Do you have any idea what it is like to live in my house where I am so scared that I spend most of my time hiding in my room, just waiting for whatever might happen next?" I was in full flow now and nobody was going to stop me. I didn't want answers and I didn't wait for any.

"Yes, that's my life. I dread leaving school every day because I don't know who is going to be my Dad's target at night. Will it be me? Or my brother? Or is my Mum going to get beaten up whilst we have to listen again? Will I have to spend yet another night in my room hearing their shouting, terrified as I hear my Mum scream for help, knowing I can't do anything to help her? Or maybe I won't even get as far as my room and just pray I can get into my hiding place behind the sofa before I get caught."

"Breathe," Mirabriel reminded me.

I took a few seconds to concentrate on my breathing. I was strong but my heart was racing. I let my breathing fall gently into place which made me feel more relaxed and gave me more strength whilst my heart had stopped racing so fast. I looked around and only a few people were looking at me. I could see the teacher out of the corner of my eye but I'd no idea what she was doing.

"Sometimes I get fed, sometimes I don't, sometimes it's safe to sleep, and sometimes it's not. This has been the only life I've ever known. I thought you all had the same life. And I thought it was normal, but I realise now I'm not normal. My life is not normal. I now know that I'm different, and being different is what makes so many people take advantage of me. Hit me. Attack me. Trip me up. Speak about me. Point at me. Being different is what makes the only safe place in the world for me an unsafe place." I could feel the tears welling up in my eyes, but I refused to let them escape.

"How do you think it makes me feel to come to school and feel just as afraid as I do at home? How do you think it makes me feel?" I looked at everyone. "Come on, someone tell me." The room was so quiet you could have heard a pin drop.

"Someone, anyone, tell me. Come on, Ben, you weren't so quiet a few minutes ago when you were laughing and calling me names, so let me hear you now. I'm listening." I looked at him. He just looked at the floor in silence.

"Dawn, let's take a few minutes outside," the teacher said in an attempt to stop me.

"Please Miss, let these people see just how the way they treat me affects me and anybody else that they may choose to bully. And I say bully because that's what it is. I get bullied at home and now the bullying in school is making me dread coming to school, so please can I have a few minutes to stand up for myself, for once in my life?"

She nodded and sat back down again.

"Thank you," I said.

"Who can tell me how you think you're making me feel when you laugh at me, talk about me behind my back and in front of me, when you trip me up?" I continued. "Lara, David, Ashley, come on - you found it very funny a few minutes ago and yesterday and the day before. What did you want me to feel? Tell me so I can understand." Nobody said a word.

"I don't know your name," I said, pointing at the boy who'd tripped me up when I'd arrived at school that morning. Everyone looked to see who I was pointing at. He just looked at the pen in his hand and refused to look at me. "But tell me, when you laughed at me and left me lying on the ground with my face pouring blood, how did you want me to feel? What did you want to achieve by doing that in front of everyone?" I looked at him with a mixture of anger and hurt. "When you called my Dad a drunk, did you not know I'm already aware that he's a drunk? Don't you know I have to hide from him when he's been drinking? I know what he does is wrong and by calling me "Daddy drunk" you just remind me of everything I come to school to forget?" I said looking right at him.

"What's the point?" I asked. "What am I even trying to achieve by telling you all this. All I'm doing is giving you even more to bully me with. Well, go ahead, I don't care anymore. I'm already broken so you can't break me anymore. I'll let you all go back to laughing at everything I've said. You can keep talking about me, tripping me up, and hurting me, because I don't care anymore. I ask only one thing – just leave my brother Danny alone. He doesn't deserve to feel the way that I do. Please don't break him any more than he is already and don't do this to anybody else. Think about what you want that person to feel and if it's not nice then don't do it. Treat others the way that you would like to be treated. None of you know what's going on in anybody else's lives at home so please be kind to others and don't make them feel the way you make me feel."

I turned to the teacher and said, "Thank you for letting me have that time," and walked back to my seat. Nobody said a word as I finished and I wasn't aware of anybody looking at me as I sat down.

"I don't know what on earth came over me, Mirabriel, but I do feel much better after that. Thank you for being there with me, it made me feel calm and strong. I felt like I *had* to do that. I'd had enough. I hope I've not let you down," I communicated through my thoughts.

"Dawn, I am incredibly proud of you, my dear child. You spoke the truth from your heart and you did it beautifully without hurting anybody. The only thing that will have hurt anyone there is the truth."

I was too busy concentrating on my breathing whilst speaking to Mirabriel to hear what the teacher said. It was something about taking notice of what I'd said, and then she told the class to take an early break.

I was aware of everyone getting up and leaving the room and I waited until I was the last one left before I got up and walked towards the door. Mrs Thomson stopped me and put her hand on my arm. She told me that I'd done a very brave thing and she thought I was a kind, strong and special person.

"I mean what I say, Dawn. If I was your Mum I'd be very proud that you were my daughter and as your teacher I can tell you that I am very proud of you. Don't ever doubt how special you are" she said with what looked like tears welling up in her eyes.

*If I was your Mum....... Her words ran through my head. I often felt guilty wishing I had another Mum, but if I had a Mum who stood up to Dad then life would be so very different and it wouldn't feel so bad. But I also knew that it wasn't easy for Mum either and it made me feel guilty for thinking that way.

"Thank you, Miss, and thanks for giving me time to speak. I'm sorry - I don't know what came over me, but I do feel better having spoken and I hope it stops them making anybody else feel bad," I muttered nervously.

"You'll probably never know the difference you've made to others, but trust me you have made a difference, Dawn," she said smiling at me, "And you can come and talk to me anytime about anything. Anything...... and I mean that, okay?"

I believed her.

"Thank you, Mrs Thomson." I smiled as I left the classroom.

Lola and Peggy were waiting for me outside. Lola gave me a big hug, something she'd never done before.

"Wow Lola, what was that for?" I chuckled, taken aback.

"Dawn, we're your best friends and we didn't know about half of those things you said in there. We didn't know how you really felt. We had no idea that things at home were so ugly," she said with tears in her eyes.

"Hey, I'm fine, I just got mad at them for laughing at me all the time and when I saw someone's foot stuck out to trip me up again, well I just snapped."

We walked towards the playground and I could feel people looking at me, but instead of staring at me

172

as I walked past they looked away to avoid eye contact, they felt awkward.

I didn't think much more about what happened in class. I'd moved on, but I guess that's just what I've learned to do in life. If I held onto the bad feelings it would be like holding a lump of hot lava – as long as I was holding onto it, I'd only be hurting myself. So I'd learned to let my thoughts and feelings go, just like letting go of the lava, and it didn't seem to hurt so badly. Instead I was learning to find peace by living in the moment I was in. When my thoughts were constantly about fear it made me feel sick. The trick Mirabriel taught me about breathing made a big difference and the more I practiced it the less sick I felt. Instead, it made me feel much more at peace with everything.

I need to teach Danny so he can also learn to cope better too I thought to myself.

"Don't worry, Dawn, we'll teach Danny tonight in the thistle house when you both come to the WOL," said a voice I knew and recognised.

"Frangel Briadh!" I said out loud excitedly.

"What was that, Dawn?" Lola asked.

Ooops I'd done it again! I chuckled to myself.

"Dawn, what are you talking about?" Peggy asked.

"Let's go play tig," I said, hoping I'd got away with it.

I could hear Frangel Briadh giggling which made me giggle too. Whenever I thought about Frangel Briadh I pictured us flying for the first time which always made me smile. I went outside with Lola and Peggy and we played tig in the playground for the rest of our short break.

The rest of the day at school was strange. I felt an odd kind of strength I've never felt before. It was as if I had control over how I felt which allowed me to show everyone I wasn't the weak person they'd thought I was. Just because my Dad is a drunk, just because he beats up my Mum doesn't make me a bad person and today I wanted everyone to know that.

There was no doubt that my strength came from Mirabriel, without her I'd never have had the guts to do what I did.

"No, Dawn, it's not down to me at all. You have the strength in you to do anything you want to do. You just need to believe it. The strength you showed today has always been in you, a little push was all that was needed for you to use it," Mirabriel murmured in my ear.

Peggy and Lola were chatting to me, so I just smiled and thanked her again. The rest of the day passed quickly and I was on the bus with Danny before I even had time to think about what might be waiting at home. This was a first for me. I don't remember a day that has gone by when I didn't stress about what might happen that night.

Mirabriel was definitely helping me by teaching me to focus on my breathing and being in each moment and although I still found myself worrying about going back home at times, I seemed to be getting better every day at taking my mind back into the moment I was in which helped me feel so much stronger.

"What happened to you today?" Danny asked inquisitively.

"What do you mean?"

"The whole school's talking about how you stood up to bullies in your class. Is that true?"

"Yes, I guess I did" I replied, feeling a tiny bit proud of myself "until today I'd not actually thought of them as bullies, but I guess they are" I finished.

"A bully is someone who makes another person feel bad about themselves, Dawn. Whether it's by calling them names, laughing at them or hitting them, it's all the same. They are trying to make you feel bad about yourself and that makes them bullies," Mirabriel said.

"That happens to us all the time," Danny said. "Oh wow, I heard you speak to Dawn," he continued in an excited voice, "even though I can't see you."

Mirabriel giggled. "I can let you hear me when there is something you need to hear. It's like when there is an emergency and I need you to hear me so you can protect yourself. I have ways of making you hear what I say. You may not hear me say the words and sometimes it may come as a thought but rest assured that I am talking to you."

"I'm not sure I totally understand. I think I do..... maybe..... kind of....." Danny said

"Have you ever gone to cross the road thinking it's okay to go when at the last minute you suddenly see a car coming out of the corner of your eye?" Mirabriel asked.

"I've done that," Danny replied.

"Me too," I said.

"Well, that is your guardian Frangel connecting with you, even if you don't hear their voice, they are telling you there is danger and giving you the feeling you need to look. That's how they protect you. That's the job of a guardian Frangel, to protect you. And everyone has one, even those who don't believe in us still receive protection from us." I found her voice comforting.

"But how can you protect everyone in the world at once?" Danny asked.

"That is a good question, Danny, and the answer is I don't. Everyone has their own guardian Frangel who protects them, just like you have your Eagle Warrior of Light.

"I've no idea how it works, but I know it does so I'm not going to question it, I'm just going to enjoy knowing I'm safe with you in my life and my Night warrior too."

Mirabriel smiled. I could see her in my mind now without her having to appear in front of me, I see her as if she is standing in front of me and I loved it.

"That's because you are becoming more in tune with my energy," Mirabriel said. "The more you focus on each and every moment, the more you will feel and see my energy and the more at peace you will be with everything in your life. Even the stuff that makes you feel bad won't feel so bad and you'll cope with it so much better."

"Mirabriel, I had no idea I could feel so positive about something that makes me feel so bad," I told her.

"That's why I continually remind you about your breathing, because that is what is helping you to be in each and every moment," she said.

"But I can't do it all the time, I don't remember. I've only remembered to do it on my own a few times, I've needed you to remind me the rest of the time," I said. "I'd love to be able to do it without you having to remind me."

"I can't do it at all!" Danny piped up.

"My dear children, tonight we are going to take you both to the thistle house and teach you more about breathing and dream walking," Mirabriel said in a cheery voice.

"But we don't know how to get there on our own," Danny said.

Mirabriel chuckled. "And that is just what we are going to teach you tonight, my sweet boy. We will come for you later. Have fun, my beautiful children." And with that Mirabriel disappeared.

CHAPTER EIGHTEEN

Danny and I just looked at each other and spent the rest of our journey home in silence, lost in our own thoughts. We got off the bus and instead of feeling the fear I usually felt, I was excited at the thought of being taught how to get to the WOL on our own. I'd love to be able to go there all by myself, anytime I felt like it.

I was so lost in my thoughts on the walk from the bus stop to the house that I didn't even notice where we were until we were home. Danny must have been the same as he didn't seem stressed the way we normally would be on our way home. As we arrived we gave each other a nervous glance before we opened the door. Mum was on her own in the kitchen, making soup. I didn't see Dad, but Mum seemed more relaxed than normal, so I took it to be a good sign. She gave us a hug as we came in and told us that Dad had nipped out, but he'd taken her to buy some shopping earlier and she'd got carrots to make soup. It was nice to see her smiling, it didn't happen very often. It was as if she really enjoyed knowing that she was giving us a treat for dinner.

I couldn't remember the last time the energy in our house was so relaxed. I surprised myself with that thought, surprised that I picked up on energy. I was becoming so much more aware of what was going on around me. I was stressing less and living more, but I knew that was because Mirabriel was around me.

"No, it's not Dawn," she said, "It's because you are focussing on being in each and every moment of your life. When you are thinking about what's happened in the past you are lowering your mood, making you feel sad. When you think about what may happen in the future, even in the next five minutes, you become stressed and anxious. So by being in each and every moment you are neither of those which mean you can appreciate what is around you at that very moment."

"Oh, I get it! That makes a lot of sense," I said realising it was out loud again!

"Dawn, who are you talking to?" Mum asked.

"Oh, just my invisible friend," I said wanting to tell her so she could learn not to stress but I should've known that she wouldn't believe me.

"Don't talk nonsense. There's no such thing as an invisible friend. Stop talking to yourself," she said.

There was no point in arguing with her as she was never going to believe me anyway, so I didn't say anymore. We sat at the table as Mum got the soup ready, we were all chatting and it was nice to feel this relaxed at home.

"Where's Dad?" I asked.

"He's gone to get some fresh bread for our soup," Mum said. "We forgot to get it when we were shopping. He's so good to us, we must show him how much we appreciate him when he gets back. Don't forget to thank him for buying the carrots and for going to so much trouble to get bread."

I remembered how much of a good mood he'd been in that morning. Things really were getting better and it felt good. I would make sure he knew how grateful I was so it stayed that way.

Ten minutes passed.......twenty minutes... an hour... Two hours and Dad still wasn't back. I could see Mum was getting anxious. Please don't let him be in the pub I thought. No, he wouldn't. He wanted to look after us and care for us and I just needed to remember that.

Suddenly there was a thud at the door. All three of us jumped. That familiar thud meant only one thing. Dad was drunk and that was him falling against the door as he tried to get in.

The door flew open and Dad staggered in. I felt sick and I knew Mum and Danny did too. It was too good to be true and I should have known it, life was so cruel. Why did we have to constantly go through this, I thought to myself.

I focussed on my breathing and tried not to think about anything other than counting my breaths.

"You're right, don't think. Your thoughts can be your enemy," Mirabriel said.

I didn't really understand what she meant but I did as she asked and I got rid of all my thoughts so I could concentrate on breathing.

"Did you get the bread?" Mum asked, trying to act normal.

"Bread? What bread? Now where's my dinner and make it snappy, I'm starving," Dad said as he slumped onto the sofa.

Danny and I took the opportunity to run upstairs before Dad noticed. On days like this it was better to be hungry than to be in the same room knowing what was coming next.

We both went into our own rooms and straight to the Amitola. I could hear Mum clattering plates and pans downstairs. She was obviously worried and stressing about getting his dinner to him before he started on her.

I wish I could teach her what Mirabriel had taught me, or maybe Mirabriel could teach her.

"Dawn, my thoughtful sweet child. I love that no matter how hard things are for you, you still think of others" Mirabriel said as she appeared in front of me. "Your Mum already has her own guardian Frangel who tries to help her, but at this time she is choosing to ignore them. She chooses to ignore some of the thoughts that are sent to help her. You have to understand that each person has their own journey to make in life and not everyone believes or wants to believe that they have a guardian Frangel. We must respect that, but even if they choose not to believe, their guardian Frangel will stay with them anyway. The only rule Frangels have is that before they can help someone that person must ask for it. If your Mum wants help to leave your Dad she must ask the Frangels for their help. Even if she doesn't use the word 'Frangel' and just says to an empty room that she needs help, it will be heard and her prayers will be answered. The only time the Frangels are allowed to step in and help without being asked is to save your life."

"But how can they speak to Mum and give her messages if she hasn't asked for it?"

"Well," Mirabriel replied, "If a big stone was about to fall on your Mum's head her Frangels would be allowed to send a warning to make her move. Everyday your Mum's Frangels will talk to her and try to get her to hear them by giving her messages, but she may choose to ignore them or tell herself it is just her imagination."

I understood exactly what she was talking about because if I hadn't seen Mirabriel with my own eyes I'd probably have thought some of the things she said to me were just my imagination.

"So I can't say or do anything to help Mum? She has to get the help when she is ready?"

"Exactly!" and with that the rainbow stars rose up around Mirabriel, forming the shape of her rainbow as she melted into it and disappeared.

I tapped three times on the Amitola and Danny appeared on the other side. He looked nervous, but I guess we both knew what was coming next.

"Danny, concentrate on your breathing" I told him. "It'll stop you feeling so nervous and it will take away that sick feeling."

"What do you mean, concentrate on my breathing? If I wasn't breathing, I'd be dead." Danny snapped. I didn't take it personally, he was only snapping because he was about to hear Dad attacking Mum.

"Danny, please trust me. Just do what I tell you and it will help." I promised.

"Okay. Tell me what to do."

I started talking Danny through the counts of breath.

"This is stupid, how is this going to stop me worrying about Mum!" Danny said in a disbelieving tone.

"I felt the same when Mirabriel started teaching me it, but I trusted her and did it anyway and it worked! If you are focussing, really focussing, on your breath, feel it come into your body and concentrate on feeling the air go out your nose, if you do that then you can't think about Mum and Dad at the same time. Please trust me and try it," I pleaded.

Danny closed his eyes and I saw him breathing more deeply. After about twenty seconds he opened his eyes and told me in a dismissive tone that it was no use, he just couldn't do it.

"C'mon Dan, just try. I had to do it loads of times before I felt it work."

"But I can't concentrate. Every time I think of my breath I just think how stupid it is," he retorted.

"And so did I," I said "but I kept trying. Don't you remember the night you heard Mirabriel telling me to keep breathing?"

"Oh yes, I do. Is that what that was all about?" he asked.

"Yes, and it does help, so come on just try it again. Really concentrate on your breathing."

Danny closed his eyes and I could see his breathing slowing down. His eyes were shut for about thirty seconds when the shouting started downstairs. I could hear Dad shouting the usual horrible names and Mum screaming. There was a crash - probably Mum being thrown against something. Danny's eyes were now wide open and he had the frightened look he always had when this started.

"Right Danny, this is when you really need to concentrate the hardest," I told him. "You need to focus on this so you won't hear the noises downstairs. I don't know how it works, but it does. Do it with me, I'll help you."

I didn't wait for him to answer, I just told him to close his eyes and started counting for him. I kept my eyes open so I could make sure he closed his and after a short time he did. I'd only counted to five twice when he opened his eyes again, but as soon as I told him to close them he did as I asked. I could hear the fighting but I knew I had to concentrate hard for Danny's sake so I just kept counting.

"Breath in, two, three, four five... hold two, three, four, five... out, two, three, four, five." I repeated this about five times and the last time Danny kept his eyes shut the whole time. He started to look relaxed, so I kept counting but closed my own eyes too.

I had no idea how long I'd been counting for when all of a sudden I was holding hands with Danny flying through the air in the World Of Light. We landed outside a huge thistle house, definitely the biggest thistle I'd ever seen. It was green around the bottom with a bright purple door and a purple roof.

Danny and I just looked at each other in disbelief. I couldn't find the words and looking at Danny nor could he.

"I don't get it..." I said. "Wow, can you believe it Dan? We did it! Oh my goodness, we actually got here without Mirabriel. WE DID IT!"

It didn't take long for the surprise to turn to excitement and Danny started to run off.

"Stop!" called a voice from a bright ball of rainbow stars that had fallen down and landed in front of us.

"Mirabriel, is that you? Did you help us get here?" I asked.

She giggled. "No, I did not my beautiful child, you did it all by yourselves."

"But how? Please tell me so I can do it again!" I demanded.

"By doing what you just did," Mirabriel replied.

"But we didn't do anything," I said feeling confused.

"Oh yes you did. You remembered your breathing?" she replied.

I looked at her in amazement. "Do you mean we got here just by concentrating on our breathing?" I asked, but Mirabriel had disappeared.

She reappeared a few seconds later on my right shoulder and Danny giggled out aloud when he saw me jumping with fright.

"Dawn, Danny, I am so pleased and proud that you have been able to trust me and do as I asked, because by doing so you have found how to remove yourself from what is going on around you and take yourselves to a better place," she said, beaming.

"You mean this is all because we are breathing?" Danny asked.

"No, sweetie, not just because you're breathing but because of your ability to concentrate on your breathing. You have been able to take your mind away from what was going on around you," Mirabriel replied. "When you focus on your breathing you can't focus on anything else, like the noise downstairs, so everything else gradually fades into the background and you can separate your mind from your body."

"So that means that if we just think about our breathing we can get to World Of Light?" Danny asked.

Mirabriel jumped from my shoulder to Danny's and it was my turn to giggle as Danny jumped. She tapped him on the head as she stuck out her tongue and his hair was covered in rainbow stars, making me laugh even harder.

"Danny, you won't get to the World Of Light by just thinking about your breathing, you have got to really concentrate on it. You need to think about your breathing and nothing else. As soon as a thought comes into your mind imagine it going into a cloud and let it blow away then concentrate on your breathing again."

I understood what she was saying, now. I remembered all the times I tried to concentrate on my breathing but couldn't do it for long enough because I always ended up thinking about something else. But the more I'd practised the better I'd got.

"Can I go play now?" Danny asked impatiently.

"Yes of course you can, but it's important that you come into the thistle house first. I have something I want to teach you." Mirabriel replied.

We followed Mirabriel as she flew in front of us to the house. I wanted to fly like her on my own, but after I'd tried it on my own without Frangel Briadh and failed miserably I'd decided not to try again.

"Have patience, Dawn, and you will soon be able to," Mirabriel said.

Arrgh! She was lugging into my thoughts again.

She giggled – as she heard my frustration. "Don't worry Dawn, I'm not going to listen to every thought you have I have my own life too, but I will hear the thoughts that I need to hear so I can help you when it's needed."

I just smiled.

We walked into a big round dark room, with lots of glistening stars on the roof. It was a bright yet dark purple colour inside. There were lots of lovely little lights twinkling around the room and lots of rugs on the floor and it felt a lovely place to be. I hadn't even sat down but I felt at home. There were benches all around the walls, covered in beautiful purple velvet cushions.

Frangel Briadh was waiting at the front door.

"Eeeek! I'm so happy to see you both here. Welcome to my home," she said excitedly. "Come on, come on, come and sit down, I can't wait to teach you both how to go dream walking!"

"How to what?" Danny asked.

Frangel Briadh chuckled. "Dream walk – that's what Mirabriel does when she takes you to the WOL. It's a kind of relaxation. I'm going to teach you how to relax properly and take yourself to the WOL or any other place you can visualise in your mind, without you having to actually be there. It lets you walk through your best of dreams and make them real and you can do this when you hear the shouting at home to help you feel less sad or in any other situation where it would help to escape from sadness around you."

"Wow, do you mean we will be able to go to the WOL anytime we like?" Danny asked.

"Yes, I do. But you don't actually have to be there in person to feel like you are there." Danny and I looked at each other, confused.

"Let me show you instead of explaining," Frangel Briadh said. "It will all become clear and make more sense once I've shown you."

She told us to pick a rug or a chair each. I chose a lovely purple rug with a matching cushion and a soft fleece blanket. Danny chose one of the benches with the purple velvet cushions. Mirabriel sat down next to me on another rug. She looked tiny on it!

Frangel Briadh put on some magic music. It was so relaxing sitting on the rug in the dark with the music, star light and all the other little lights around the room. I could easily have fallen asleep.

"Now I was about to tell you both to get comfortable, but it looks like you have done that already," she giggled. "Do either of you want anything before we start?"

We shook our heads. I didn't know what was going to happen but I was excited because everything we'd done so far was fun so I thought this probably would be too.

"Come on, kiddos. Let's do this!" she said. "All I am going to ask you to do is to follow my voice. You can keep your eyes open or closed, it's up to you."

Mirabriel jumped up and sprinkled glitter, first over me and then Danny and told us to relax and enjoy. We looked at each other and giggled. I lay back and closed my eyes.

"Well, it looks like you pair are ready to go. Let's begin."

I opened my eyes for a few minutes, focussing on the stars on the ceiling as I listened to Frangel Briadh's soft voice.

"Dawn, Danny, this is your time my beautiful children, so please enjoy it. Start to notice your breathing. Become aware of the breath going into your lungs and back out through your mouth.

"Really focus on it. If a thought comes into your head, just think about your breath. Imagine your breath is a beautiful bright white light which you are breathing in. Imagine the light is going all around your body, filling every part of you including your fingers and toes, then imagine it coming back out through your mouth. Next time you breathe in count to five, visualising that white light going all around your body. Then hold your breath for five before letting your breath out for five, visualising the air leaving your body. If you have bad thoughts, imagine them leaving your body in a black cloud, then breathe in that bright white light to replace the black. Keep focussing on your breathing and let your mind go to where I'm going to take you."

I did as she told me and I became very relaxed. I imagined all the worry about Mum and Dad coming out of my breath in a black cloud and I imagined the bright white light filling me with love and happiness. The more I did it the more I could feel my body relax.

Frangel Briadh kept speaking. "As you focus on your breathing I want you to imagine you are sitting on a large rug. I want you to look at the rug carefully and see what colours and patterns you can see. Don't tell me, just see it in your mind. As you sit down on this rug I want you to imagine it's starting to lift off the ground with you still sitting on it. As it lifts higher and higher you feel lighter and lighter, until you are so high off the ground that you are floating on the rug far above the World Of Light. Look at everything beneath you, look at the details of everything you can see, look at all the people you can see. If a thought comes into your mind, just go back and focus on your breathing. As the rug moves over the WOL I want you to see what is below you. It doesn't have to be anything you have seen already, you can use your imagination. Look at the details and focus on what you feel as you breathe in the smells. Allow yourself to feel as if you are really up there. Feel the air on your skin, feel the heat of the sun on your face and feel the wind blowing through your hair. Can you see what is below you? Can you feel the excitement of knowing you are up above the rest of the world? Sit on your magic rug for a few minutes and enjoy the scenery beneath you and around you, feel the cold wind on your face. Take in every shape and colour and just lose yourself in the peaceful feeling it brings you. Really feel as if you are living a dream that you would love to be real."

After saying this Frangel Briadh was silent for what seemed like a long time.

I felt myself exactly where she described. I was on a magic rug and I really could see the World Of Light below me as I floated and it felt very real. I saw two unicorns beneath me, I caught their eye as I flew over them. I saw Jeremiah and we looked at each other as we connected. It felt beautiful.

Eventually, Frangel Briadh spoke again. "Now see your magic rug lowering back down to the ground, very slowly. Slowly.....slowly, take yourself back to the rug sitting on the ground. As the rug rests on the ground become aware of your breathing again. Feel your breath coming in through your nose, out through your mouth. Feel your body sitting on your chair or lying on the ground and become aware again of your fingers, your toes and of your body making contact with the ground or the cushion. As you become aware of the noises in the room, become aware of your surroundings and when you feel ready open your eyes."

I did as she asked and I felt so relaxed. It really felt as if I'd been where she'd taken us – over the World Of Light. She left us in silence for a few minutes then told us when we were ready we could sit up. I felt so relaxed I could easily have lain there for hours, but after a minute or two I sat up. I looked around for Danny and he was sitting up too, looking very refreshed, as if he had been relaxing for hours.

Frangel Briadh asked how we felt and I was aware that we were all smiling. Danny said that he couldn't stop his mind from thinking at the beginning, but each time he had a thought he did as she'd said and it went away again. He told her that by the time he'd been over the WOL on the magic rug he was able to follow exactly what she said and he felt as if he was there too. Frangel Briadh seemed very pleased that we were both able to do it.

"Now you both know that no matter where you are, or what you are doing, if you just stop and concentrate on your breathing you'll be able to take your mind anywhere you want to go. You can imagine you are on a beach or in a forest. Anywhere you want to believe you are, you can be. You just need to do what I did there just now," she said soothingly.

"This will help you cope with any difficult situation, whether you're at home or at school, or indeed anywhere at all," she added.

"Thank you for teaching us Frangel Briadh!" I said.

"Yes… thank you," Danny stammered.

"You're both so welcome," she responded. "I'm very proud of you both."

We were all beaming with happiness and joy. The feeling was nice and I felt relaxed, happy and safe. I loved it! I hoped I'd be able to go Dream walking when I was on my own.

"Of course you will my sweet," Mirabriel said. "Just have faith and trust in yourself."

"Oh, I love you Mirabriel!" and she smiled as she told me that she loved me too.

We had a glass of water - Frangel Briadh said it was good for helping you stay grounded so you didn't feel like you were floating after you had been on a magical journey. She also said it's good to stand outside and feel your feet on the grass and imagine roots growing from your feet down deep into the ground which will help you feel strong, especially in difficult times. She knew so many different ways of coping when things felt hard, and they were all so simple to do!

We went outside. It was so bright that it took a few minutes for my eyes to adjust. We stood on the grass and did as Frangel Briadh had described. I imagined feeling roots grow from my feet going deep into the ground, helping me stand strong. As I was doing it I thanked Frangel Briadh, through my thoughts, for all she had done for Danny and me.

We stood on the grass chatting for a few minutes before Mirabriel told us we could go and enjoy more adventures in World Of Light. She said she'd make sure we were back in bed before Mum or Dad came looking for us.

Danny took off to wherever he'd decided to go as soon as Mirabriel said we could go. I knew I could trust her, she always had us back in our room in time, so I decided to go and visit the gnomes in the gnome pod behind the thistle house - they looked so cute. I'd spotted them earlier but I didn't have time to visit.

I skipped off towards them. They looked very friendly as they sang and danced while working in their gnome garden, each with an important job to do. It looked as if they were happy as they whistled, sang and chatted. I said hello and asked if I could help. They were friendly and seemed excited that I'd asked. One introduced himself as Jack the Gnome. He was the sweetest little gnome, with the cutest little red cheeks and a cheeky smile. He seemed to be the cheekiest one there as I heard him telling the other gnomes to hurry up and work faster as he sat on a little toadstool and ate a bowl of soup. He had lots of food next to him including a huge bag of chocolate and it didn't look like he'd planned on sharing it with any of the other gnomes. From the way they all laughed together I imagined the other gnomes would soon make sure they got some if they wanted it!

I found a quiet spot in the corner of the pod and I sat for a few minutes giving thanks in my head for all the good I had in my life. I decided to try and speak to the Rockflower to see if I could persuade him to change so he could find smiles in his life too, instead of misery. After a short time of focussing I changed my jumper to the rainbow jumper and saw images of him running through my head as he ran around the Warton Pod. I also heard him plotting his next sabotage in the WOL. *You will never learn will you?* I spoke through my thoughts to him. I clearly gave him a fright but he spoke back very quickly and told me he wanted to change. He said he really wanted to be a good person. I told him if he did he would have to look into the enchanted water to which he quickly agreed, telling me that he would do anything he could to be a good person.

"How do I get him there?" I called to Mirabriel.

"Be very careful my dear child, these Wartons will pull any trick to destroy the WOL." she warned me.

"I know Mirabriel, but if he doesn't truly want to change he won't be able to get through the iron gate, will he?" I checked with her.

"No, my dear, you are quite right he won't. He has to truly want to change and mean it from his heart. His words can fool some but his energy never can" she replied.

And with that Mirabriel did her stuff as I watched the Rockflower appear outside the black iron gate. I could still see his black aura and it didn't feel nice I thought to myself as I realised I was feeling his energy, but I wanted to try and help him so I thought it only fair to give him a chance.

"Mirabriel he definitely won't get through if he doesn't mean it, will he? I would hate for him to harm anything or anybody in the WOL" I told her.

"Fear not, bad energy can never get through that gate" she reassured me.

I watched him for a few minutes as he paced nervously around the gate. "Where am I? Where are you? How do I get through to that magic water?" he asked.

"You have to truly want to change and if you don't and you are trying to trick me you will end up back at the Warton pod. You cannot trick us like you think you can" I told him. "Now close your eyes and send lots of loving, healing thoughts and prayers to the animal kingdom" I instructed him.

A few seconds later he was back in the Warton pod and I was back at home in my bedroom as I heard footsteps at the top of the stairs.

CHAPTER NINETEEN

It must be Mum, I thought, as Dad would be too drunk to get up the stairs without loudly bumping into the walls. I was sitting on top of my bed with my clothes on. I quickly picked up a book so Mum would think I'd been reading.

She walked into my room and asked me if I was okay.

I nodded, looking at her face which was bruised. She'd obviously been crying for a long time. She was always covering for him, I had no idea why when he treated her so badly, but she always did. I heard the same excuses again and again. As she got closer I couldn't look at the mess he'd made of her face, I looked away. It upset me to see her like that and I couldn't stop my tears from falling.

"Mum, you're in a mess again. Why do you let him do that to you? You don't need to put up with it. We could get out of here and have a happy life and you'd be safe. We don't need him in our lives. You know we can get help to get out of here, why don't you ask those people who can help?" I pleaded.

We heard Dad staggering up the stairs.

"Hurry up, get into your bed and pretend you're sleeping!" Mum panicked.

I lay down and pretended to be asleep. I heard Dad and Mum meet at my bedroom door. There were sounds of a scuffle with muffled sounds of Mum trying not to scream. I lay on my bed, wishing I could help her when I heard Mirabriel plead with me to dream walk. I closed my eyes and concentrated on doing everything I'd been taught in the thistle house earlier. I focused on my breathing and imagined myself in a cave until I actually saw and felt myself in the cave. The more I concentrated on being there the more I felt like I was there. The cave was made of purple satin inside and there were lots of candles lit everywhere. It made me feel safe, as if I was protected from the world.

Suddenly I heard Mum shouting, but I kept my eyes closed and went back to concentrating hard. I managed to go back into my cave again – my new safe place. I could smell the fresh sea air and feel the wind on my face. I knew I wasn't really there but it felt as if I was. I was lying on my bed, in my cave, when I heard Danny screaming at Dad.

"Leave her alone you bully. Just leave her alone!"

I jumped up and ran into the hallway. Dad pushed Danny against the wall, telling him to go back to bed. Danny let out a yelp and pushed back, hitting his fists off Dad's back and shouting at him to leave Mum alone. Dad had hold of Mum with his other hand, but before I could pull Danny away, Dad swung around and hit him on the side of his head. He screamed in pain - with the force Dad used it must have really hurt him. Before Danny had a chance to have another go I pulled him away and dragged him into his bedroom.

"And stay in there!" Dad slurred after him.

"Danny, are you ok?" I asked stroking his hair.

He was so angry. I'd never seen him that angry and I felt a little afraid. I didn't want him going back out to Dad and I was scared Dad would come in here.

"Dan, please, please calm down or he'll come after you!" I begged.

"I don't care! I'm sick of it! He's nothing but a bully!" Danny screamed.

"Yes I know, but please calm down or you'll make him worse," I pleaded again.

I held him close to me, stroking his hair and back, trying to soothe him and calm him down. He slowly responded and started to calm. I could hear Mum pleading with Dad to leave us alone then the sound of a slap and Mum's stifled yelp. I felt Danny get uptight again.

"C'mon Danny, focus on your breathing. I know you don't feel like it, but please try. Breathe in white light, breathe out anger." He started to do as I asked but I could feel him letting his thoughts get in the way.

"Danny, every time a thought comes into your head focus on your next breath," I reminded him. "In... two... three... four... five, hold... two... three... four... five, out... two... three... four.....five." I helped by keeping count for him and only closed my eyes after Danny closed his. I kept counting and after a few minutes we were back in World Of Light again.

"Wow! Danny we did it again!" I shrieked with excitement.

Danny had changed from being raging mad to happy, relaxed and excited. We saw two elephants as they scooped us up in their trunks. At first I shrieked but then I laughed - it was so much fun! I sat on his trunk and my elephant lifted me up to his head. He held me there as we looked into each other's eyes, it was as if we were having a conversation without saying a word. He lifted me higher until I was alongside his back. He made a noise and I realised he wanted me to climb on. I clambered over and sat up there looking around me. It was amazing! It was a pod I'd never been to in the WOL before. I could see giraffes and zebras, all looking so friendly. Danny was also sitting on an elephant's back and we started to move.

"Yikes!" I squeaked before giggling.

As the elephants walked Danny didn't say a word, he just kept smiling. I ducked as we went under a tree – it was pretty high up there on the back of an elephant! As I ducked I grabbed a bunch of leaves which I fed to a giraffe that came right up beside me. Even though he was massive, he was also very gentle as he ate his leaves and carried on walking past us.

The sky was blue and the sun was shining. We were in a huge open space with lots of trees, zebras and giraffes and little ponds of water. As the elephant moved I saw dolphins jumping in a river. I felt excited and happy but more than anything I had the feeling of being at home in this place, and I somehow knew Danny felt the same.

Another giraffe walked towards me. I showed him my hands and said, "I've no leaves left, I'm sorry."

"That's okay," the giraffe said.

"Oh my goodness, did you just speak to me?" I shrieked.

He moved his lips in a funny way saying, "Yeah, I sure did." And he walked away.

"Danny, did you hear that?" I shouted.

He kept smiling. "Yes I did," he chuckled.

I looked above us and saw a rainbow over our head – we were in the purple. I knew it and I loved that stripe.

As we got closer to the large rock pools, I noticed one had a waterfall with two sea lions huddled underneath it.

"Wow. I love seals," Danny called over to me.

"Hey, dude, mind your language. We're sea lions, not seals," one of the sea lions grunted in a most unimpressed fashion. Danny's mouth fell wide open and he was speechless. That was a first.

"Are you all able to talk?" he asked, with the look of shock still on his face.

"Of course we can talk, but only you can hear us," one of the sea lions chipped in.

This was so much fun. It made life at home seem so much easier to deal with.

"Where are we going?" Danny asked me.

"I don't know. Wherever the elephants want to take us." I was unable to stop smiling.

"Where do you want to go?" my elephant asked as it pushed his trunk up in front of me.

"Do you have a name?" I asked.

"Yes, of course I do" the elephant trumpeted, "Don't you humans have one too? Anyway, I'm Sandra and it's great to have you on board."

"Oh it's so good to meet you, Sandra. Thank you for taking us on this beautiful journey."

"Would you like to meet the monkeys?" she asked.

"Yes! Oh, yes please!" Danny and I said at the same time.

"Just be warned they can be very cheeky," Sandra said, which made it sound like even more fun. We walked past lots more trees and little rivers. I suddenly thought about Mirabriel and Frangel Briadh and wondered why we hadn't seen them.

"Because you don't need to, you are doing just fine on your own" came a familiar voice in my ear."

We got close to a forest and I saw three monkeys swinging from tree to tree in the distance.

"Are you sure you're ready for this? You really wanna do it? These guys can be very mischievous," Sandra warned again.

"Oh yes, nobody could be cheekier than Danny," I giggled.

"Oi, watch it you!" he retorted, sticking his tongue out at me.

Because we were so high on the elephant's backs, we could see into the middle of the trees as we got closer.

THUD!

"Ouch!" I screeched. There were three monkeys hanging from a tree giggling. I'd been hit on the head by a banana that one of them had thrown at me! Another one had a banana in his hand and I saw him getting ready to throw it.

"Duck!" I shouted to Danny.

"What duck? I can't see......OUCH!" he shouted as the banana hit him square on his head.

Sandra and Danny's elephant both put their trunks up towards us. At first I got a fright until I realised they only wanted a banana. I reckon they had a deal with the elephants that if they took a visitor to the monkeys so they could have fun with them, by hitting them with bananas, then the elephants would be rewarded with a banana for themselves. Sounded like a good arrangement to me. If I was an elephant I'd probably agree to something like that too. I loved this place. It was so peaceful, fun and safe.

I looked over and saw the dolphins still jumping in the water. "Sandra do you think the dolphins would let us swim with them?" I asked.

"Yes, I do believe they would," she said as she started stomping her way as gracefully as she could towards them.

"C'mon Dan, follow us!" I shouted back to him.

We got to the dolphins and Sandra let out a loud noise. Two dolphins jumped up into the air. "I have two people who would like to swim with you, would you like some company?" she trumpeted. The dolphins let out a high pitched noise and Sandra told us that meant yes. She raised her trunk and told me to sit on it so she could lower me down. Danny's elephant did the same and we ran straight to the water to swim with the dolphins. As I reached the water I realised I hadn't thanked Sandra or said goodbye. I turned back but they'd started walking away.

"Wait!" I shouted after them. "Thank you for all you've done for us."

They looked back and raised their trunks, made a loud trumpeting noise and continued on their way. I went back over to Danny who was already racing through the water holding onto a dolphin's fin. He was laughing and looked very much at peace. I went to go into the water but stopped, wondering whether I should take my clothes off, but before I had a chance to decide a dolphin swam right up to the edge of the water, put his nose towards me and urged me to jump on. I held onto his fin and thanked him as we started to ride the waves and zoom about the water. Being with the dolphins gave me a peace that was unfamiliar outside the WOL. I can't explain it any other way, it was just a beautiful peace. I loved feeling so close to the dolphin, I could really feel his energy and it felt nice. The feeling I got as I rode with the dolphin was as if we were one, as if we were joined together, and I loved it. Just the way it felt with Jeremiah.

Just as I was having the time of my life I found myself tucked up in my bed and a few seconds later Mum came into my room asking if I was okay. I nodded as she stood looking at me for a few minutes, so I closed my eyes and pretended to go to sleep so she would go away, which she did.

I must have fallen asleep as the next time I opened my eyes the morning light was coming into my bedroom. I jumped up in a panic and looked at the clock. It was 7.15 am. I got Danny and myself ready for school and was dreading going downstairs but there was no need because when I got there nobody else was up, which was a welcome relief for both of us.

I went to get us a banana each for our breakfasts as we were about to leave for school, but there weren't any so we went to school hungry again.

"Hurry, let's get out of here before he wakes up," I said to Danny.

We walked to the bus stop in silence. Danny hadn't said a word since we left the house but he began talking very excitedly about the night before in the World Of Light. He spoke about all the animals and how much he wished he could have stayed. As he spoke I looked at him and noticed a mark on his face.

"Oh Danny, you have a mark on your face where Dad hit you!" I told him.

"Oh no! What if someone notices?" he asked in a panic.

"Then tell the truth, Danny. Margaret told me that he wouldn't keep getting away with it." I tried to persuade him. "We can't keep protecting him forever. Each time we tell a lie to cover for him we're giving him the message that it's ok to do this to us, so if you're asked please tell the truth and don't cover for him."

The school bus was getting closer and we had to run to make sure we didn't miss it. It was a close call, but we made it to school on time. We went our own ways and said we'd see each other after school. The morning at school passed pretty quickly. I didn't see Danny, but at lunchtime Mr Mackintosh asked me to go to his office. I knew what it was about before I even got there.

I waited at his office for ages and, when he eventually appeared, he left me sitting in his office again, just like he did the last time. It made me nervous as I remembered my last experience. When he finally came back he asked me what things were like at home. I didn't want to tell him as he didn't really help me last time, so I asked him where Margaret was and told him I'd speak to her.

He mumbled something I couldn't hear before picking up the phone asking somebody to contact Margaret. When he put the phone down he told me he cared and was worried about me, but he must have known I wouldn't speak to him as he went on to tell me that Margaret was on her way and wouldn't be long.

He left me sitting outside his office while I waited for her. She appeared a short time later and smiled when she saw me. I jumped up as soon as I saw her, giving her a hug which she returned. I really trusted her and she knew it. She told me she would be back in a few minutes and she went into Mr Mackintosh's office.

When she appeared about five minutes later she said she was taking me to the nurse's room to have a chat. When we got there she asked how things were at home. I told her the truth and she looked sad. She asked about Danny and I told her that he was okay. She didn't ask about the night before when Dad hit him so I didn't mention it. I asked her if things would change at home and she said she was doing all she could to make sure I was safe. Because I trusted her I didn't question this. She told me I would be seeing her the following week and I went back to class.

Later that afternoon I met a different police lady and the bull nose lady in Mr Mackintosh's office. They put on that video recorder again as they asked me questions about home, just the way they did before. I told the truth about what happened to Danny the previous night. I didn't feel so nervous this time. I just trusted that they would do all they could to help us.

When the bell went for home-time I made my way to the bus stop, as usual. As I got near to the gate I noticed the boy who had previously tripped me up, causing my nose to bleed, standing to the right of it. I didn't know his name and I had no intention of speaking to him, but he knew my name and called it out as I got closer. He waved his hand as if he wanted me to go to where he was standing.

"Dawn, I just wanted to apologise to you. I know what I did was really mean and I am sorry. At the time I thought it was funny, but only because I didn't really have any friends and I thought that I would make more friends if I made people laugh. I did make people laugh and I did make more friends, but what I know now is that I also hurt and embarrassed you. After you spoke to the class, lots of people refused to be friends with me again. Until you spoke in class I had no idea what you were going through and I will be totally honest and tell you that I thought you were just a weird kid and I'm sorry for thinking that. You have taught me not to judge people and to treat others the way that I would like to be treated myself."

I was stuck for words. I wasn't expecting that and I didn't know what to say. Part of me was annoyed that he deliberately tripped me up, just to make others laugh at me, but I also knew how hard it must've been for him to apologise to me like that.

"It's okay, as long as you don't do it to anybody else." I said with a confidence that surprised me.

"Dawn, I can give you my word that it will never happen again. You have shown me that it feels much nicer to be nice and I am grateful to you for teaching me that."

"Thank you for telling me this.... ermm.... I'm sorry, I don't know your name."

"Dave. It's Dave."

"Thank you for apologising Dave. I need to run before I miss my bus." I said as I started to walk away, smiling inside knowing that I had actually helped someone find their beautiful.

"Thank you Dawn" he shouted after me.

I got to the bus stop just in time. Danny was sitting in his usual seat and I sat beside him.

"How was your day?" I asked.

"It was okay. I got asked about the mark on my face," he said looking worried.

"What did you tell them?" I asked.

"The truth."

"Good, we can't keep protecting him, Danny, I'm proud of you" I told him.

"They told me that they weren't going to keep us away from the house like they did with you before. They said things were going to be fixed, but they didn't say how."

We chatted about anything and everything on the way home. Neither of us wanted to have time to think about what might be waiting for us. We got off the bus and started to walk home as normal. As we got closer to the house we both went quiet, dreading what we were going to find when we got there. Before we got to the door Mum opened it and came running out to meet us.

"Hurry!" she said, as she ushered us in the door.

I was afraid. She'd never met us at the door like this and certainly not in a panic. When we got inside Mum told us to follow her upstairs. Danny and I looked at each other then raced upstairs with her. She went into my bedroom but kept looking out the window onto the street as if she was waiting for someone. I assumed it was Dad that she was looking for. She must have paced back and forth to the window about five times, sweeping her hair off her face as she did. I could see sweat on her forehead and she looked very worried. After she checked out the window one more time she handed me a carrier bag and told me to get all of my clothes out of my cupboard and put them in the bag. I did as she asked. I don't have many clothes so they all fitted in the one bag.

"What is going on, Mum?" I asked feeling scared and nervous at the same time.

"Dawn, Danny, I'm taking you out of here once and for all. What you went through last night should never have happen to either of you. It's not fair and it's my job to protect you," she said looking flustered. "We need to leave as soon as possible before your Dad gets home and catches us. If we don't leave, social work are going to take you both away from me to keep you safe. They took your Dad into the police station this afternoon before you got home from school. But they didn't know how long he would be in there for. They told me that they would make rules for him that he didn't come home or near us after they let him out of the police station, but just in case he broke those rules they wanted me to make sure I got you out of here after you got home from school. I'm so sorry, I should have done this long before now."

She paced back and forth to the window a few more times as she pulled out my underwear from the drawer and got me to put them in the bag too. Danny and I looked at each other, shocked, excited and confused all at the same time.

"What, how, why?" I asked. So many questions were going through my head. How could we escape him without getting caught? There is no way he would obey those rules, he would come back for sure. Where were we going to go? Would he find us? We'd really pay for it if he did. I had so many things going through my head but the thought of getting out of there was enough to make me just do as Mum told me to.

"Dawn, we don't have time for questions, we need to get a move on. Come on, quickly," she said. "I have got to get you both out of here."

"But Mum, aren't you coming with us?" Danny panicked. "I'm not going anywhere without you."

"Of course I am coming with you, but if your Dad finds out what we are doing it won't be safe for any of us," Mum said, still pacing back and forth. "I've been speaking with a lady from Women's Aid and she's been helping me since you told the police and social work what happened the first time, Dawn. She's spoken with me lots and I know that the way your Dad treats us isn't normal and shouldn't happen. She's made me realise that there is a way out and she can help. She's shown me that I have strength I never thought I had to get us all out of here to start a new life, where you'll be safe and happy. I want to see you both smile instead of seeing fear on your faces all the time." Mum was crying as she spoke. "I wanted to do it before now, but social work have left me with no choice. I am very proud of you both for being able to speak up and tell the truth. I'm sorry I haven't been able to be that strong. Now I am forced to protect you and I now need to find the same strength that you have both found. Thank you for helping me. So please, Danny, run and get the clothes out of your cupboard and take them through here, I can't leave the window in case your Dad comes home. But be quick. Our lift will arrive in a few minutes."

She kept looking out of the window as we waited for Danny to come back with his clothes. "It's here!" she said. "Our lift has arrived! Hurry Danny! Dawn, here's another bag, grab anything else you want to take. We won't be coming back here again so what you leave behind will have to stay."

I was excited yet scared. A lift out of here! That was more than I ever imagined to be possible. Mum kept looking out of the window. I didn't stop to look out, I was too busy gathering all the things that meant a lot to me, like my teddy that I'd had since I was a baby. The one I held onto when I was scared.

Danny came back through with an armful of clothes but just as he was about to put them into the bag Mum screamed at us to put everything back in our wardrobes as quickly as we could as Dad was coming down the road.

My tummy leapt and I just wanted to cry. "Mum, what about our lift, can't we just run to the car now?" I begged. "Please let us just get out of here."

"Dawn, the lady giving us the lift must have seen Dad. She's driven away. She knows how dangerous it would be for him to catch us. You have got to hide, do you hear me? I have to tell Dad that you are not here, do you both hear me? Do you?" she demanded. We nodded, scared and so disappointed that we were about to escape once and for all but now that chance had gone.

"I promise I'll get us out of here, but please stay up here and hide in Dawn's cupboard and take this, I got it from the lady from Women's aid, call the police on 999 if you hear me shouting LEAVE" as she gave me her mobile phone and locked the cupboard door that Danny and I hid in so Dad couldn't get to us. She ran downstairs in time for the front door to open.

We tried not to breathe to make sure we didn't make any noise. We were petrified. I heard Dad ask what she was playing at and she told him that "the kids" had been taken by social work. I heard him get angry and I hovered with my finger on the 9 button of her mobile phone as I waited to hear the word she told me to listen for. I heard her telling Dad that she loved him and of course she wanted him to stay. She told him those bail conditions were nothing to do with her. I didn't know what that meant but then I heard her tell him that it wasn't her choice to have him live somewhere else or for the kids to go elsewhere. I got the feeling that bail was the rules he had been given by the police not to come to the house. I felt sick when I heard her tell him that she wanted him to stay and that she wouldn't tell the police that he was there. She sounded like she really meant it, but I also wondered if she was trying to trick him as I knew she couldn't leave us locked in a cupboard for long. I just kept hugging Danny and telling him we would be ok. Having the mobile phone helped us feel a bit safer and I kept my finger on that "9" all the time.

We must have been in there for at least an hour when we heard footsteps running up the stairs. We both panicked, froze and tried not to breathe again. If that was Dad we were for it I thought as I pressed 9 once. But it was Mum's voice I heard as I heard the cupboard door unlock. She told us that Dad had gone to the pub. Mum took the mobile phone from me and called the lady who was helping us leave. Mum told us that she was on her way to pick us up. Danny and I both burst into tears and ran to hug Mum.

"Come on both of you, we don't have long to get out of here." She started the pacing back and forth to the window again. "If there's anything you want take it now. Just be quick as the lift will be here in a few minutes."

I couldn't quite take it in. I wanted to ask so many questions, especially where we were going, but I knew it was not the time. Our priority had to be to get out before Dad got back. Once we'd got all our things into our bags we stood and looked at Mum, still not really believing that we really were about to leave.

Downstairs as we got to the front door we heard a car door slam. All three of us froze, looking at each other in sheer terror and panic. If Dad caught us now, with our bags in our hands about to leave, we'd all get it.

Mum had frozen to the spot and couldn't move.

"Mum!" I shouted.

She ran to the kitchen window and let out a huge sigh of relief while bursting into tears at the same time. "It's only the postman. He's late today. Now let's get going," she said.

She opened the front door and the postie was standing there. "I think this is for you, young man." he said, handing Danny an envelope. Danny was so excited I think he forgot that we were leaving. He rarely got mail. In fact, I don't think he'd ever got mail before.

"Danny, now isn't the time, come on take it with you," Mum said. "We need to get out of here." She looked out of the kitchen window again. "Right – go! Now! Come on let's go," and she pushed us out of the front door.

Danny had already ripped his letter open and started jumping up and down.

"I won! Mum - I won!" he shouted.

"Danny, whatever you've won will have to wait. Now hurry up and get over to that red car as fast as you can," Mum said.

"But Mum... I won the zoo competition!" he shouted whilst running over to the car. He looked happier than I'd ever seen him looking in his entire life. Even happier than in the World Of Light and that was saying something.

Danny and I looked at each other as we both heard Mirabriel whisper, "I told you, all you need to do is believe." We smiled as we stood beside the red car with Mum.

We all turned back together to look back at the house. We were about to be free for the first time in our lives. We turned away and got into the car that was waiting for us. Waiting to take us to freedom.

Sitting in the back seat of the car I heard Mirabriel telling me to close my eyes. I did as she asked and I saw the Rockflower standing outside the black iron gate again. Wow I thought to myself has he really decided to change or is this another attempt to trick us. I visualised my rainbow jumper so he couldn't see me "Hey Rockflower why are you here again, you know your energy can't trick us?" I reminded him.

"I don't want to keep hurting and frightening others" he informed me "When you talk to me it scares me as I can't see you which has made me realise how much I must be frightening others. I don't want to be that kind of person anymore. Please help me" he begged.

"If you want to change then you have to do this yourself. I am going to leave you here and if you mean what you say then send out some loving prayers for the animal kingdom. If you're sincere I will see you at the enchanted water. If not, you will be put back to the Warton pod." I directed him and opened my eyes again.

"I can't wait to go to the WOL again" Danny piped up excitedly in the back seat as I kicked his shin and gave him the look that told him to be quiet.

"Danny I told you we are not ever going back there again, so you won't be playing on the garden wall, not in that house anyway" Mum said.

Danny and I looked at each other and giggled.

I closed my eyes again and saw Rockflower standing over the enchanted water. "You've got to look into the water, but you have to do this yourself, nobody else can do it for you" I told him as I noticed his black aura was replaced with a beautiful white aura all around him.

I so badly wanted to tell him to look into the water and persuade him to change, but I knew it had to be down to him to choose which path he took in life. After a few seconds he looked into the water which immediately started spinning. It got faster and faster as it formed a rainbow which began wrapping itself around Rockflower in a spiral tornado of rainbow colours. I jumped as I saw a burst of white light come out of the middle of the rainbow where Rockflower had been and a few seconds later a beautiful robin appeared out of the middle of it. The robin picked up an end of the swirling rainbow and started to fly away with it. The whole rainbow had unravelled and there was no sign of Rockflower. I felt very pleased with myself, knowing that I had helped Rockflower want to change and find the beautiful inside of him. Maybe now I could help Mum do the same, I thought to myself.

I opened my eyes and sat smiling as we made our way out of our street.

"Wow kids, look at that beautiful rainbow" Mum said as she pointed to the sky ahead.

The following pictures were drawn by children from Women's Aid when they were asked to draw a picture of their "Happy Wonderland."

"Ch, Age 10"

"Girl, Age 13"

Anonymous

"Male, Age 10"

Anonymous

"Boy, Age 11"

Anonymous

"9"

"Girl, Age 12"

"Girl, Age 10"

"Boy Age 11"

"Girl, Age 9"

"Girl, 11 yrs. M"

"Female, Age 8"

Anonymous

"Boy, Age 8"

"Boy, Age 9"

BUDSTER OF THE YARD

Buddy was a real police dog who was given to the police after he had been found living in horrible conditions. When he was found he had long straggly hair, he was yellow and smelly because of cigarette smoke and he was very scruffy.

After a haircut, a bath and eight weeks of training Buddy became a qualified, hardworking, police dog, who loved to work. He also loved his handler and his family, who all adored him. His tail wagged as long as he was awake and his favourite game was looking for his ball.

Thank you Buddy, for all your hard work, for dedicating your life to working for the police and helping make our world a safer place. Thank you for the smiles you brought to so many people every day.

Acknowledgements

Gratitude is very important to me, so I do not apologise for the length of the acknowledgements section. It is from my heart that I would like to thank the following people, who without their support and input this book would not be in your hands today:

My beautiful friend Dawn, who has believed in me and this book from the start. Without your encouragement this book would never have made it to the end. I love you to innffiinniittyy aanndd beyyooonndd.

Elizabeth for all your support, guidance and belief in this book. You have been a true inspiration and a good friend. Thank you.

All of the children from Women's aid who drew pictures of their happy wonderland. Thank you for all your hard work, I hope you enjoy seeing your pictures in this book. Be proud of the strength you find to get through every day.

Jolie for the strikingly perfect cover of this book and for the long hours and devotion you put into getting it just right. You've been a joy to work with and a good friend. Thank you.

Paul, Ruthey babes, Jane, Mairi, John.S, Faye & Suzanne for all the hours you put into proof reading this book. Your hard, dedicated work is greatly appreciated. Thank you all.

Flora Napier, blueprint editing, whose editing & proof reading was invaluable in the early stages of this book.

Thank you to the anonymous author of the "Travelling Angels" story which I found online. This story helped me get across a very important message to our next generation of children.

Buddy for his loyal service to the police and for making our world a safer place. Your unconditional love will always have a special place in the hearts of those who were blessed to share their lives with you.

Neil for your timely size tens which gave me the final push to get this book into the hands of those who need it. Thank you for your friendship and unrelenting belief in me and this book. Unicorns & rainbows.

Craig who has been a hero in real life and is one of life's brightest shining diamonds. Thank you for your invaluable friendship.

Richard for his selfless dedicated work at "For The Right Reasons" publishing group and to his team for their hard work, commitment and the strength they find every day to make a positive difference to themselves and to others.

DJNL, Mairi, Ruthey babes, Jane, Katie, Sonya and Jacqueline for your priceless friendship and belief in me. I love you all and treasure you all.

Michele and John, for always being there for me, for knowing me, believing in me, supporting me and for all those smiles as we danced the nights away. I love you.

Isobel for being the best adopted Mum I could ever have asked for. You were my role model growing up and I only hope that I have even half of the beautiful heart that you have. I love you.

John Stack for teaching me about the roses. Thank you for not only proof reading the book and giving me your personal & professional opinion, but also for your friendship and unrelenting belief in me. You're never allowed to retire!

Stewart and Tracey for helping me turn a page in my life, enabling me to find my true potential and follow my dreams. Thank you doesn't say enough.

Ramsay for your support in helping me progress this book. Without your help I'd never have found a friend in Elizabeth and Richard, whose help has been invaluable. You're a shining light & all the work you do is invaluable. Thank you for all you do for everyone.

M.B for never giving up on me. Thank you for your help, support & never ending patience, which has been invaluable.

G, J, A, AA, GA & S.G – My eternal thanks for your guidance, support & unconditional love. I love you always.

Domestic Abuse – What to do if you need help

If you, or someone in your family, like your Mum, is being hurt you should first of all make sure you can get to a place that is safe for you. Then call the police (999) and tell them what is happening. When you call they will ask for your name and address so they can send a police officer to your house to help you. Make sure you do not hang up the phone until the police arrive, that way they can hear what is going on and talk to you whilst you wait for them. If you are worried about one of your friends, then it is important that you tell an adult. That could be a teacher or someone else you trust. Remember it is not your fault. If someone chooses to hurt another person then you cannot change them, they have to want to get help themselves and it is not your fault if they do not want to get that help. There are lots of numbers at the end of this book that you can call to talk to somebody that can help support you.

SOME FACTS ON DOMESTIC ABUSE

Alcohol does not cause domestic abuse, but it is widely recognised as an aggravating factor. There are many cases of domestic abuse where alcohol is never involved. At no time is alcohol ever an excuse, or a reason, for a person to be violent, or abusive, to another. Violence does not have to be present for domestic abuse to take place. Males or females can be responsible for domestic abuse and it can happen in any relationship, regardless of age or religious beliefs.

This book has been written using my broad experience of working with children who have lived with domestic abuse and focuses on a fictional family as an example of domestic abuse, where the male is responsible for the abuse and alcohol is an aggravating factor.

If you know alcohol makes you violent or abusive, you should abstain from alcohol until you seek professional help. There is a list of useful resources at the end of this book where both victims and perpetrators can access help and support.

On average a woman is assaulted 35 times before her first call to the police (Jaffe, 1982)

In 90% of domestic violence incidents in family households, children were in the same or next room (Hughes, 1992)

20% of children in the UK have been exposed to domestic abuse (Radford et al, NSPCC, 2011)

Resources

The following numbers can be used for information, support and guidance. All information relates to the UK. The internet is a valuable resource for further information relating to support within and out with the UK.

Police
Emergency – 999
Non-emergency – 101
Crime stoppers - 0800 555 111
www.crimestoppers-uk.org

ChildLine
0800 1111 – 24 hour, 7 days a week, Freephone number (landline and mobiles).
www.childline.org.uk

Get Connected *(16-25 year olds)*
0808 808 4994
www.getconnected.org.uk

NPSCC *(National Society for Prevention of Cruelty to Children)*
08088005000 - 24 hours, 7 days a week.
88858 – Text
www.nspcc.org.uk

Scottish Women's Aid
0131 475 2372
www.scottishwomensaid.co.uk

Women's Aid Federation of England
0117 944 4411
www.womensaid.org.uk

Welsh Women's Aid
02920 390 874
Wales Domestic Abuse Helpline
0808 80 10 800
www.welshwomensaid.org

Shakti Women's Aid
Edinburgh: 0131 475 2399
Fife: 01383 431 243
Stirling: 01786 464 004
Dundee: 01382 207 095
www.shaktiedinburgh.co.uk

National Domestic Violence Helpline
0800 2000 247 - 24 hours, 7 days a week,
Freephone number (landline and mobiles) which is
run in partnership between Women's Aid and
Refuge.
www.womensaid.org.uk
www.refuge.org.uk

Northern Ireland Women's Aid
02890 331 818
www.niwaf.org

The Haven Project *(Wolverhampton)*
01902 572140
www.havenrefuge.org.uk

Muslim Community Helpline
020 8904 8193
www.muslimcommunityhelpline.org.uk

Jewish Women's Aid Helpline
0800 59 12 03
www.jwa.org.uk

Chinese Information and Advice Centre
020 7692 3697
www.ciac.co.uk

Samaritans
0845 7909 090
www.samaritans.org.uk

Victim support
0808 168 9111
www.victimsupport.org.uk

Parentline Scotland (Advice & support for a child)
0800 282233
www.children1st.org.uk

Men's Advice Line (for men experiencing domestic violence)
0808 801 0327
www.mensadviceline.org.uk

Respect (for perpetrators of domestic violence)
www.respect.uk.net